TALES OF THE DARK FOREST

GOODKNYGHT!

Other titles by Steve Barlow and Steve Skidmore

TALES OF THE DARK FOREST

GOODKNYGHT!

STEVE BARLOW & STEVE SKIDMORE

ILLUSTRATED BY FIONA LAND

Collins
VOYAGER

An imprint of HarperCollins*Publishers*

First published in Great Britain by CollinsVoyager in 2001
CollinsVoyager is an imprint of HarperCollins*Publishers* Ltd,
77-85 Fulham Palace Road, Hammersmith,
London W6 8JB

The HarperCollins website address is
www.harpercollins.co.uk

7 9 8 6

Text copyright © Steve Barlow and Steve Skidmore 2001
Illustrations by Fiona Land 2001

ISBN 0 00 710863 X

The author and illustrator assert the moral right to
be identified as the author and illustrator of the work.

Printed and bound in Great Britain by
Clays Ltd, St Ives plc

The Legend of the Dark Forest

According to legend, the Dark Forest was not always dark. Long ago, the Kings of the Forest ruled a rich and fertile land from their high throne in the great City of Dun Indewood. Their prosperous and peaceful realm was defended by brave and honourable Knyghts, and you couldn't throw a rock without hitting a beautiful maiden, a sturdy forester or a rosy apple-cheeked farmer. (Of course, none of the contented citizens of Dun Indewood would ever dream of throwing rocks about anyway; and if they did, one of the Knyghts, who were not only brave and honourable but just and kindly too, would ask them very politely not to do it again.)

It was a Golden Age.

But over the years, the Knyghts and Lords of the City grew greedy, idle and dishonest, and fell to quarrelling among themselves. The line of the Kings died out.

The power of Dun Indewood declined. Contact with the other cities and towns that lay in the vast wilderness of the Dark Forest became rare, and then was lost altogether when the Forest roads became too dangerous to travel.

The creatures of the Forest became wild and dangerous until only a few hardy souls dared to brave its perils. The citizens of Dun Indewood continued to argue among themselves and cheat each other, turning their backs on everything that happened outside the City walls.

With no one to tame it, the Forest became home to truly dreadful things. Beasts with the understanding of men, and men with the ferocity of beasts, roamed the dark paths. The trees themselves became malevolent and watchful. And the Forest *grew*…

Well, that's the legend, anyway.
Of course, these days, nobody believes a word of it…

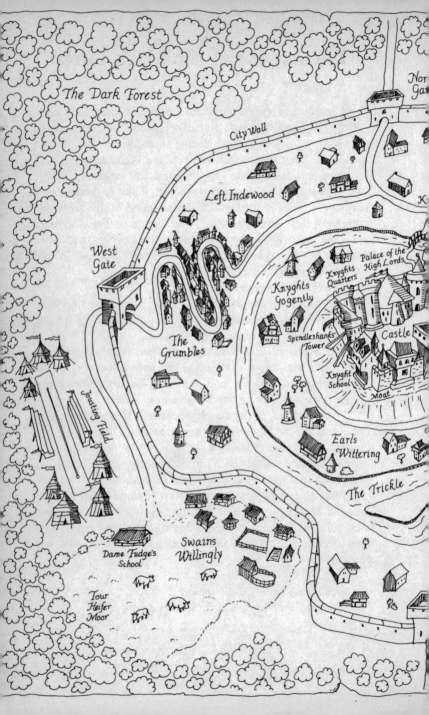

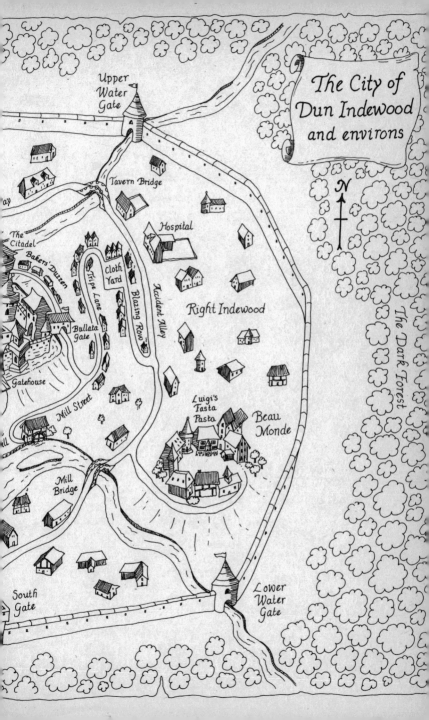

CHAPTER ONE

How Willum the Swineherd was Tanned most mightily on his Backside by cause of Lord Symon's Dishonesty and how Both encountered a Wolf in Creep's Clothing.

Doctor Blud frowned at Symon. "I am going to have to punish you most severely," he said.

Symon nodded. "Yes, sir."

"You have been bad." Doctor Blud gave an experimental lash with his cane. It sliced through the air with a swishing noise. "Very, very bad."

"I know, sir," said Symon smugly.

"It is therefore," Doctor Blud went on sternly, "my sad duty to deliver a thrashing you will never forget."

Symon's grin threatened to split his face in half. "Of course, sir."

"Very well." Doctor Blud pointed to the punishment stool. "Willum – bend over."

Will gritted his teeth. He walked stiffly to the stool and knelt before it. Symon gave Will a sorrowful smirk. "You know," he said, "this is going to hurt me more than it hurts you."

Will gave Symon a long, slow, angry look. "I don't think so."

Symon's leer grew even wider as Will took a well-chewed roll of rags from his belt pouch, and clenched it between his teeth. Then he bent over the stool.

Doctor Blud raised his cane...

THWAAACK!

"That's for scrumping Farmer Porl's apples..."

THWAAACK!

"...and that's for putting Goodwife Loosey's cat in a bag..."

THWAAACK!

"...and that's for putting Goodman Tobey's ferret in with it..."

The list went on, with a lash for every one of Symon's wrongdoings. Breaking windows, stealing, telling lies – the supple cane whistled down and raised a small cloud of dust from the seat of Will's britches.

Eventually, the cane splintered. Doctor Blud leaned against his desk, breathing hard. "Very well," he panted. "We'll leave the cock-fighting and smoking behind the stables for next week." As Will staggered to his feet, still silent in spite of the tears coursing down his cheeks,

Doctor Blud pointed the shattered cane at Symon. "And I hope that will be a lesson to you!"

"Oh, yes, sir," said Symon with a delighted grin, "it certainly will. Thank you very much."

"You are dismissed, Willum." Doctor Blud sank into a comfortable chair and prepared to take a well-earned rest. Will put his roll of rags back into his pouch and turned to go.

"Not so fast!" Symon was suddenly at his side, speaking in an urgent whisper. "I've got a job for you."

"Oh, yes?" Will, rubbing his backside, gave Symon a very unfriendly look.

Symon glanced at Doctor Blud, who was settling down for a snooze. He grabbed Will by the elbow and dragged him into the next room before he judged it safe to speak. Then he said, "Hoop-legs Horris."

"Your coachman?" Will looked confused. "What about him?"

"He's got an attack of the marthambles."

Will shrugged. "Too bad."

"He can't drive – can't hold the reins. I want you to do it." Symon cut off Will's spluttered protest. "I've seen you drive the farmers' carts into the City."

"Farmers' carts pulled by oxen are one thing, a coach pulled by four horses is a bit different..."

"You'll manage. Anyway, Horris will be there – you just do what he tells you."

"Why should I?" objected Will. "And where will you be?"

Symon gave him a haughty look.

"Jervaise deLacey and I will be inside the coach, naturally, with... ahem..." Symon flushed. "With two ladies."

Trust Symon to use his father's coach to try and impress girls, thought Will. Then a horrible suspicion struck him. "Where are you planning to go?"

Symon waved airily towards the window. "Out there, of course."

Will stared through the window in horror. "Into the Forest? You must be mad!"

Will and Symon were standing in one of the upper rooms in the castle. Spread out below the walls, with its cobbled streets laid out like a map of itself, was the City of Dun Indewood. Its cramped, tumbledown buildings seemed to huddle together for protection, like a flock of sheep surrounded by wolves. Outside the City walls were scrubby farmlands and untidy villages. And beyond them...

Beyond them, a sea of green swept, unbroken, to every horizon. Leaves in all hues from almost-yellow to wine-bottle green rippled in the morning breeze like waves in restless motion. From where Will stood, the shimmering canopy of trees looked harmless enough. But beneath it, the Forest floor lay hidden from sight, an unknown world of terror.

Infants in their cradles were told horrible stories of the perils of the Forest. Children were threatened with it. "If you do that again, I'll leave you in the Forest," exasperated mothers would cry. Their children would stick their tongues out and pretend not to care, but they would stop misbehaving, at least for a while.

Will shuddered. The Dark Forest was inhabited by wolves and bears, which occasionally raided the farmlands surrounding the City; but these were the least of its dangers. Ogres, giants, dragons and worse were said to lurk in its trackless depths. The Dark Forest was full of perils to chill the bravest heart. It marched on and on to the end of the world, and every inch of it was strange, grim and treacherous.

"People don't go into the Forest," said Will apprehensively. "They say that any who do, don't come back."

Symon snorted. "Nonsense. Old wives' tale."

"You wouldn't call it nonsense if you lived outside the City walls." Will's home was in the village of Swains Willingly, which lay between the City and the Forest. He had seen some of the things that came out of the Forest, and heard about plenty more. "Anyway," Will went on with more assurance, "you're not allowed to go into the Forest. They'll stop you."

"Who will?"

"The guards."

Symon raised his eyebrows and gave Will a superior smile. "You mean my father's guards?"

Will hesitated. Symon was the son of High Lord Gordin Mandrake, ruler of the City of Dun Indewood. Would the guards stop the High Lord's son, the True Acorn of the Mighty Oak, the Lord of the Leafy Glades, the Warden of the Green Reaches (and a dozen other titles that Will couldn't be bothered to remember)? Would they dare?

"If anything happened to you," said Will (rather hoping that something would), "Lord Gordin would kill me."

"I order you to drive us into the Forest!"

Will shook his head.

"If you refuse," said Symon nastily, "I'll do something so bad that Doctor Blud will beat you to a jelly. Have you forgotten that you're my whipping boy?"

It wasn't really a question. Will's bottom was smarting fiercely from the latest session with Doctor Blud's cane. It wouldn't surprise him if it glowed in the dark. He sighed. He really didn't have much to lose. And, he had to admit to himself, he really would like to try driving a coach and four.

"All right," he agreed heavily.

"Excellent!" Symon reached for his sword and his cloak. "Let's go for a spin in the woods!"

The coach rattled through the winding streets of Dun Indewood with Will at the reins. He'd found an old cushion to pad the hard driving seat, but he still winced painfully as they clattered over the bumpy roads. Hooplegs Horris, the castle coachman, sat next to him – a small man with bow legs and a ferocious squint. He smelled of stables and the tavern, and seemed to be under the impression that he was giving Will a driving lesson.

"Left hand down a bit there, lad – check behind you

now – signal a right turn, good, slow down, watch for oncoming traffic – and round we go…"

Will ignored the running commentary. He found that driving the lively, intelligent coach-horses was quite easy compared to handling the slow-witted oxen he usually had to steer. In any case, Hoop-legs Horris may have been unable to hold the reins, but he seemed to have no difficulty holding a hip-flask, from which he refreshed himself pretty frequently.

He also ignored the comments floating up from inside the coach. Symon and his friend Jervaise deLacey, shamelessly showing off for the two giggling, preening girls they had invited, were shouting pointless and contradictory instructions to Will.

"Left at the next corner, coachman."

"Go right, you fool, right!"

"Speed up!"

"Slow down!"

"You handless clod!"

"You mindless oaf!"

Will ignored them. There was no point in losing his temper. Symon could make his life a misery (even more of a misery, Will corrected himself), and Jervaise was a violent bully. More to the point, both were rich and privileged, and Will was as poor as the pigs he tended, when he wasn't being stunt double for Symon's behind.

The coach quickly passed through the districts of Earls' Wittering and Knyghts Gogently, where the nobles of the City lived. The cobbled streets were lined with grand houses, each protected by high walls, strong gates and ferocious dogs.

Further down the hill, the streets grew narrower and more crowded, and the air was full of the cries of stallholders and shopkeepers selling their wares.

"Murdles, git yur loverly Murdles."

"Gizalook! Gizalook!"

"Fresh chicks! Going cheap!"

"Woteveryawantigotit! Woteveryawantigotit!"

"Notashillin', notapenny, gis a groot an' it's yours!"

Will drove on through Bakers' Duzzen ("Hot cakes, git 'em 'ere. Hot cakes, selling like hot cakes!") and Bullata Gate and Tripe Lane with their rows of butchers' shops ("Stomachs, brains, intestines, kidneys. Offally low prices!"). The coach clattered through Cloth Yard, where Dun Indewood's tailors sat on benches outside their shops, sewing busily away ("Broadcloth! Get it while it's broad!") and Blazing Row, which echoed to the hammering of blacksmiths beating iron on their anvils ("New – *Clang* – iron!" "Any – *Clang* – shape!" "New – *Clang* – iron!" "Any – *Clang* – OW!"). Then past the hospital at Accident Alley and the students' quarters on Know Way, and suddenly they were bowling through the City gates, gathering speed as they rumbled across the scrubby pastures outside the walls. Moments later, they were driving between trees. The coach was inside the Dark Forest.

Will grinned, all his former nervousness forgotten. This was wonderful! The whip of the leaves as they brushed the side of the coach, the reins in his hands, the horses at his command, the wind in his hair...

Hoop-legs Horris cleared his throat. "Now," he said urgently, "when I slap my fist against the dashboard, I want you to bring this ve-hicle to a stop as fast as you can."

SLAP!

Startled, Will hauled on the reins and heaved on the brake. The horses reared furiously, flailing hooves scattering stones and clods of earth. There were roars of anger and squeaks of alarm from inside the coach.

The coach skidded to a halt. The horses shifted nervously, sweating and shaking their heads. Will turned to Hoop-legs Horris for approval and saw that the coachman was staring straight ahead. His lips were trembling.

Will followed his gaze – and gasped with shock.

An enormous wolf was standing in front of the coach. It was right in the middle of the road, blocking the way.

"Well, hellooo there!" it drawled.

Will blinked in disbelief. It had to be a wolf. Everything pointed to the fact.

Brownish-grey fur.

Long, wicked-looking muzzle with cold, wet nose.

Drooling fangs.

Pointy ears.

Black mask.

Black mask?

Will rubbed his eyes. The wolf was definitely wearing a mask. And a frock-coat. And a three-cornered hat, a ruff and knee britches which had obviously been tailored for someone whose legs bent the other way. And it was talking.

The wolf folded its paws. "Well, what have we here?" it said smoothly. "A coach full of rich Lordlings from Lord Gordin's court, out for a little drive in the Forest."

Four terrified faces stared out of the coach windows.

"'Going for a spin in the woods' – isn't that what you call it?" the wolf continued pleasantly. "I suppose you think it's frightfully daring?"

Will was no coward; he had dealt with wolves before. Wolf packs never came near the City, but occasionally a lone wolf would come out of the Dark Forest to try and pinch one of Will's pigs. A good biff from Will's quarterstaff usually made it change its mind. But a talking wolf was quite outside Will's experience. His hand inched towards the cudgel the coachman kept under his seat.

The wolf sauntered round to the coach window and gave a mocking bow.

"Greetings, travellers," it cried. "Stand and deliver! Your money or... what was it now? Oh, yes..."

It grinned, showing rows of razor-sharp teeth, and Hoop-legs Horris fainted.

CHAPTER TWO

H ow the Wolf was put to flight by a
Rose with sharp thorns and of What
Followed in the Woodcutter's Cottage.

T here was a sound of wailing from inside the coach. Symon's voice squeaked, "What are you going to do with us?"

The wolf sighed. "I'm a Highwaywolf – what do you think I'm going to do? I'm going to hold you up, of course, and steal all your jewels and valuables – unless you refuse to give them up, in which case I shall be forced to tear you to pieces." It shrugged. "I might do that anyway. As for your coachmen..." The wolf looked up at Will and grinned again. "After I've robbed the coach, I might gobble them up or I might let them go." It licked its chops. "Depending."

There were squeals of terror from inside the coach. Symon and Jervaise (helped out, Will couldn't help noticing, by very unladylike shoves from a couple of female feet) tumbled out and drew their swords. Knees knocking, they faced the Highwaywolf.

The wolf raised its hackles. It growled deep in its chest, a growl that became louder and higher until it was a terrifying snarl. It leapt forwards. The two young men dropped their swords and threw themselves down in the dirt, howling with terror. The wolf gave an amused chuckle and sauntered up to the coach.

It leaned casually against the door and looked through the window. "Now, I do hope you ladies are going to be reasonable. I hate to eat a big meal so early in the—"

It got no further. With a yell, Will grasped the heavy wooden cudgel from under his seat and leapt at the wolf, swinging as hard as he could. The wolf gave a howl of rage. It side-stepped, easily avoiding Will's wild swing, and cuffed him on the side of the head with a swipe from its paw. The blow sent Will flying into a tree trunk. He fell, dazed and bleeding heavily from a gash on his forehead.

The wolf prowled towards him, lips pulled back in a ferocious snarl, teeth bared. It stood poised, ready to leap...

"Hello, wolf."

The wolf froze, rigid with shock. It made a little noise in its throat that sounded suspiciously like a whine. Then it stepped back, its face twisted in horror. Will blinked in astonishment. Something had scared the ferocious creature out of its wits.

The wolf turned round slowly and gave a little whimper of despair. Standing behind the wolf was a young girl, about Will's age. She was wearing a leaf-green cloak and a bright, friendly smile.

"Fancy seeing you here," she said cheerfully.

The wolf gave another whimper. The girl pulled the cloak aside and suddenly she had a double-action, self-loading, automatic miniature crossbow in her hands, which she pointed unwaveringly at the wolf.

The quaking creature tried to pull itself together. "Oh, it's *you*. What are you doing here?" it protested in a shrill whine.

"I saw these people drive into the Forest and I thought, I do hope nothing bad happens to them on the way home. So I hung around to see that you didn't."

The wolf snarled feebly. "That's not very sporting."

"Sporting?" The girl gave the wolf a hard stare. "Well, what about you? What are you doing here?"

"Oh, just taking the air." The wolf stuck its paws in its pockets and made a ghastly attempt to look unconcerned. "You know, I almost didn't recognise you. What happened to that red cape you used to wear? The one with the hood?"

"Oh, come on. Nobody wears those now." The girl tossed her head dismissively. "Anyway, I grew out of it ages ago. My Grandmama sent it to the Society for the Care of Distressed Gentletrolls."

"Ah." The wolf cleared its throat nervously. "And how is your Grandmama?"

"Fine. No thanks to you."

The wolf gave what it probably hoped was a winsome smile. "And your dear Papa, the woodcutter?"

"A bit restless actually. He was up all night sharpening his axe."

The wolf went cross-eyed trying to see the crossbow bolt, which by now was pricking the end of its nose. Its cool exterior was evaporating as quickly as a snowflake in a furnace.

"Look, little girl," it whined, "I'm a wolf, for heaven's sake. I'm just trying to make a dishonest living; is that too much to ask?"

The girl's eyes glinted and her voice took on a steely edge. "Now listen carefully, wolf," she snapped, "because I'm only going to say this once. Stay off my turf. This is a respectable neighbourhood and we don't want it getting a bad name because of some no-good, low-life wolf with ideas above his station and no fashion sense. Do I make myself perfectly clear?"

The panic-stricken wolf nodded and stabbed itself in the nose. It gave a howl, backed away a few paces, turned and made a dash for the cover of the trees. Will could hear it crashing though the Forest as it frantically tried to put as much distance as it could between itself and the girl with the green cloak, who watched it out of sight with a ferocious scowl. "Little girl!" she muttered to herself disgustedly. "Huh!"

There were screams from the coach. The powdered faces of the two young ladies appeared at the window, shrieking at Symon and Jervaise who leapt up, grabbed their swords and scrambled for the door. Hoop-legs Horris stood up unsteadily, and with a hoarse cry clambered back to the driver's seat. The experience with the wolf seemed miraculously to have cured his marthambles. Without waiting for Will, he whipped the horses into a gallop from a standing start, and the coach careered dangerously down the road towards the safety of the City.

"Nice friends you've got."

Will turned to see that the girl was staring straight at him. He was not sure whether to be pleased or insulted by the elaborate unconcern with which she lowered her crossbow and slipped the safety-catch back on.

"What's the matter with you?" she demanded. "Don't you have more sense than to come into the Forest without an escort?"

Will was feeling shaken and his head hurt. "Never mind me," he returned hotly. "What are you doing all alone in the Forest?"

The girl gave him a sardonic look. "Discouraging the local riffraff and saving your skin. Listen, here's some really good advice. Why don't you go back to your little friends and stay nice and safe inside the City. You won't last five minutes in this girl's Forest, believe me!"

Will glared. "They're not my friends," he snapped. "And thanks for the advice." He turned his back on the girl and set off purposefully down the road.

The girl grinned. She grinned even harder when Will caught his foot in a root and fell flat on his face. She slid the crossbow into a pocket inside her cloak and helped him up.

"Your head's still bleeding," she said. "You'd better come back to my cottage and I'll patch you up." Without waiting for Will to agree, she set off into the trees. "By the way," she called over her shoulder, "my name's Rose. What's yours?"

"Mind your head."

Will ducked obediently, and followed Rose through the low doorway. The woodcutter's cottage was well made, with strong timber walls and a roof of wooden shingles. Each window was a carefully carved lattice of oak, with small panes of hartshorn. Shafts of light lanced on to the sanded and polished wooden floor.

At one end of the cottage, a figure sat tending the fire. He had the hunched shoulders of an old man, and the hand with which he reached for another log from the basket by the hearth was wrinkled and blotched with age. In spite of the warmth inside the cottage, he wore a cloak wrapped tightly around his thin body, and a hood that completely covered his face.

Will nudged Rose. "Who's that?"

"Just a traveller." Rose fetched a wooden bowl and poured cold water into it from a pitcher. She took a cloth from a nail and dipped it in the bowl. "Hold still."

"Ow!"

"Don't be such a baby." Rose scrubbed heartlessly at

the dried blood on Will's face until it, and his wound, were clean. She took white linen strips from a chest and wound a bandage round his forehead. Ignoring Will's stammered thanks, she bustled about setting wooden bowls and spoons on a rickety table.

Will sat quietly, barely taking his eyes off the old man.

"Hey, ugly!" a voice snapped from the stranger's corner. "It's rude to stare!" The old man stirred. A foot shot from beneath his robe and kicked an oddly-shaped bag lying against the wall by his stool. "Ow!" the voice sounded aggrieved. "Why don't you keep your big, flat feet to yourself, sourpuss?"

Will stared at the hunched figure. "Is he all right?" he asked in a low voice.

Rose followed his gaze. "He looks all right to me."

"No, I mean... is he safe?"

"He is in here." Rose jerked her head to the Forest surrounding the cottage. "Out there, he could be in trouble."

Will gave Rose a stern look. "You shouldn't let people into your home if you don't know who they are..."

"Oh, really?" Rose gave him an amused glance. "Well, I don't know who *you* are. Suppose you were lost in the Forest, and you saw a light, and there were things after you, and your only hope was to take shelter in this cottage – would you be happy if I said you couldn't come in because I didn't know who you were?"

"But something could happen to you," said Will weakly.

"I hate to point this out, but I'm not the one who was being hassled by the local wildlife a few minutes ago." Rose carried the bowls to the fire and filled them with greenish-brown liquid from a pot simmering on the hearth. She handed one to Will. "Try this."

"What is it?"

"Nettle soup."

Will sniffed the concoction suspiciously. "It smells disgusting."

"It is disgusting." Rose cut a hunk of coarse bread off a loaf on the table and passed it to him.

Will paused with the soup bowl halfway to his mouth. "What's in it besides nettles?"

"Do you really want to know? You'll like it better if you don't."

Will sipped the gloopy concoction. It tasted worse than it smelled. "Eeeurgh! Do you eat this sort of thing all the time?" He took a mouthful of bread and nearly choked. "What's this made of?"

"Acorns." Rose glared. "This *is* the Dark Forest, you know."

Will put his bowl down. "But aren't there..." he waved his hand vaguely, "...rabbits and pigeons and... er, stuff you can hunt for the pot?"

"Oh, yes," said Rose darkly. "You can shoot some little fluffy bunny – as long as you're very, very sure it isn't a witch's familiar and she won't turn you inside out and hang you from a tree." She wagged the bread knife at Will. "There are things out there you won't find in any of your City recipe

26

books; and some of them, if you biff them on the head, don't have the sense to stay biffed. You don't want to put something in the pot if you have to sit on the lid and hold it down until it's cooked. Anyway," Rose went on, ignoring Will's horrified expression, "it's not a good idea to concentrate too hard on hunting your dinner, because while you're doing that, chances are, something else will be hunting you."

Rose's Forest-wise air was beginning to get on Will's nerves. "Well, I didn't see anything very frightening on the way here."

"Really?" Rose looked genuinely surprised. "You mean you missed both the ghouls? And the phooka? The fachan? The redcap? I can't believe you didn't spot the nucklavee."

"I might have done," said Will defensively. "What did it look like?"

"Horse-shaped, with one fiery red eye, flippers instead of hooves, and a man's body growing out of its back with long arms that reach the ground, and a huge head that rolls from side to side as if it's about to fall right off – oh, and it hasn't got any skin so you can see all its muscles and stuff, and watch its black blood running through its yellow veins."

"No," said Will slowly. "I'm sure I would have noticed."

"Don't worry. They won't hurt you as long as you're with me. I know my way around the Forest," Rose went on matter-of-factly. "After all, I've lived here all my life."

"I didn't think anyone lived in the Forest."

"Not many people do," conceded Rose. "Just a few pigheaded types who don't like high walls and stupid rules. It's not so bad. Most of the things that live hereabouts are all right, as long as you let them know who's boss."

"That wolf seemed pretty scared of you," admitted Will.

"Oh, him." Rose wrinkled her nose dismissively.

"I didn't know wolves could talk."

"Real wolves can't. But that's the trick round here, you see, knowing what's real and what isn't. There are animals that look like humans, and humans that look like animals, and loads of things that are neither one thing nor the other."

"I'd always heard there were some pretty strange creatures in the Dark Forest..."

"Yup, the woods are full of them." Rose grinned at Will. "So what were you doing in the Forest with those stuck-up wasters anyway?"

Will scowled. "Symon made me drive the coach in here."

Rose gave him a scornful look. "Do you always do what this Symon tells you?"

Will gave her a look that mixed shame and defiance. "Mostly. I don't really have a choice. I'm Symon's whipping boy."

There was a clatter from the corner of the room as the old man dropped the poker on the hearth.

CHAPTER THREE

How Will returned home to a Further
Tanning upon his rear and how all his
Hopes were dashed.

"**W**hat's a whipping boy?" asked Rose.

"Nobody's allowed to beat Symon, because he's the High Lord's son and he's going to be the next High Lord. So when he does something bad, they beat me instead."

Rose stared. "What's the point of that?"

"Well, you see, they make Symon watch me being beaten for all the bad things he does. He's supposed to feel guilty enough about me getting hurt, so he'll behave himself in future."

Even as he spoke, Will's mind flew back to the day, many years before, when Lord Gordin's men had come to his home village of Swains Willingly. They were looking for a whipping boy for Symon, who had recently been invested as the new heir to the High Lord. The Town Crier had stood in the middle of the village green and read the proclamation. It had gone on for ages with lots of "whereas"es and "thereby"s, but what it boiled down to was that every family in the village that had a boy the same age as Symon Mandrake was expected to volunteer him for the job, or else.

From one point of view, it was an enviable position. The boy who was chosen would be sent to Dame Fudge's Elementary School. The chance to learn to read and write was not often given to Dun Indewood's poorest families, but the heir to the High Lord couldn't be expected to associate with ignorant riffraff. On the other hand, there was a pretty serious downside…

When the boys had been assembled by their hopeful parents, Gordin's steward had gone down the line pinching their arms and looking in their mouths as if they were horses. At last he had paused in front of Will.

"What's his name?"

Will's mother had dropped a curtsey so deep she'd practically sat down. "Willum, so please Your Graciousness."

"What does he do?"

Will's father was tugging at his forelock hard enough to make his eyes water. "He looks after the pigs, Your Highness."

"Is he a good boy?"

Will's mother wrung her hands. "Oh, yes, an't please Your Worshipfulness. He's the best boy a mother could have."

The steward had raised his voice. "Then be it known that

from this day forward, Willum the Swineherd shall be the whipping boy to Symon, heir to the House of Mandrake, the True Acorn of the Mighty Oak, Lord of the Leafy Glades and Warden of the Green Reaches..."

The steward rambled on, listing another dozen of Symon's titles, before continuing. "Every week, the aforesaid Willum shall report to the mighty Castle of Dun Indewood to stand punishment for his gracious benefactor, be it never so cruel; to be beaten, thrashed and whipped to within an inch of his life as occasion demands."

Will hadn't liked the sound of that, but his parents had flung themselves at the steward's feet, beside themselves with gratitude. "Oh, thank you, Your Holiness. Such an honour..."

So Will had gone to Dame Fudge's school to begin his education. And every week, he had presented himself at the castle to suffer for Symon's sins. There were always plenty of sins for him to suffer for. Symon made certain of that.

"I bet it doesn't work."

Rose's voice jerked Will back to the present. He snorted. "Of course it doesn't! Symon *enjoys* seeing me getting thrashed. It just makes him think of even worse things to do, so I get beaten even harder next time."

Rose's expression was a mixture of pity and scorn. "Why do you put up with it?"

Will sighed. "Because Lord Gordin promised my parents that if I became Symon's whipping boy, I should follow him to Knyght School."

"And that's good, is it?"

"Oh, yes." Will's voice was quiet and firm. "I've always wanted to be a Knyght. To wear armour, and ride a white charger, and protect the City and have adventures in the Forest..." Will realised he was going on a bit and finished lamely, "Well, that's what Lord Gordin promised."

"I wouldn't trust that man as far as I could throw him." Rose sniffed. "My dad says a lot of people came to the Forest when Gordin became High Lord. A few of them are even still alive. He sounds like a really nasty type." She frowned. "But messing about in the Forest is just going to get you killed and eaten; in that order, if you're lucky." She nodded towards the brooding trees beyond the window. "Take my word for it – it's a jungle out there."

Will opened his mouth to argue about Rose's choice of words; Knyghts did not "mess about" in the Forest. Then he thought better of it. "Thank you," he said.

Rose nodded shortly and started fussing about with the bowls and spoons.

"I really should get back," Will told her. "I'll be late as it is."

Rose reached for her cloak. "I'll see you to the edge of the Forest..."

"There's no need..."

"That's all you know." Rose fastened the clasp of her cloak. "That wolf may still be hanging around. He may be stupid, but he's very persistent."

It was dark by the time Rose returned to the cottage. She took a stool from the table and went to sit by the old man who was still hunched, silent and lost in thought, over the fire. Quietly, she said, "Did you catch all that?"

The hooded figure nodded.

"Didn't the runes say...?"

"They did." The old man's voice was troubled and uncertain. "He may be the one I seek. Time will tell."

"Or," said a voice from the bag at the old man's feet, "he could just be a half-baked pipsqueak who's got nothing to do with anything. Can we go to the City now?"

The old man glared at the bag. "Cease thy vexatious muttering, thou insufferable knave!"

"Well!" said the voice in scandalised tones. "Was there any call for that? I don't *think* so!"

The hunched figure turned towards Rose. Bright, sharp eyes glittered in the depths of its hood. "He must go back to the City. He must go to Knyght School."

"Wouldn't he be safer out here with us?"

The old man shook his head. "He cannot learn what he needs to know here. He will be watched in the City."

"By you?"

"And others. I shall make arrangements."

Rose sighed. "It'll be tricky. But if you're sure about this..."

The hooded figure nodded.

"He's always sure," said a muffled voice from his feet. "Doesn't it just get on your nerves?" The old man's foot lashed out savagely. "Ow! That hurt!"

"It was meant to, thou irksome idiot!"

It had not been a happy homecoming.

Rose had left Will at the edge of the trees near his village. They had walked in silence and their goodbyes had been awkward. Will had hurried home, but even so, he was late, and his father was in a bad mood because he'd had to look after the pigs himself.

"I'll teach you to go gadding about in the Forest," he roared.

"Oh, you shouldn't teach him things like that, Father." Will's mother wrung her hands. "He might do it again."

"It wasn't my fault," protested Will. "Symon made me…"

"Oh, that's right! Blame it on Lord Symon, what's been so good to you! Of all the unnatural, ungrateful…"

Will was stung. "What have I got to be grateful to Symon for? I hate him!"

"Hark at him, Mother!" Will's father frowned threateningly. "He'll be tellin' us he hates Lord Gordin next."

Will's head hurt and he'd had enough. "Well, I do hate him! He's greedy and cruel and selfish."

"I won't have you saying that about our Lord."

"Why not? It's true!"

"He's a good man. He lets you go to the castle."

"Only so I can get beaten."

"You watch your lip," warned Will's father. "He's a good master, I'm telling you. He is our appointed ruler and we are not worthy to lick his boots."

"Who says we're not worthy?"

"Well, er... he does!" Will's father's shout of triumphant laughter gave ample proof that his brains, like his teeth, were in short supply.

Will clenched his fists in frustration. "All right. Give me an example of when he's been good to us."

Will's mother squirmed as his father flapped about for an example of Lord Gordin's goodness. "Er well, er... Right! Right! What about last week! When he come out here huntin'. He said 'Good morning' to me as easy as you like."

"And then he rode over your turnips and trampled them into the mud," Will pointed out.

"Well, yers..."

"And then he rode over you."

"He's harsh, I'll grant you that. Harsh, but fair."

"He's a real gentleman," agreed Will's mother.

Will rolled his eyes. "I'm going to bed."

But Will couldn't get to sleep. He lay awake for hours, listening to the soft sounds of the pigs snuffling in their pen outside; and further off, the rustling of the wind through trees, and the strange, unearthly cries of the creatures of the Dark Forest.

THWAAACK!

Doctor Blud leaned against his high desk and clutched at his heart. Or at least, thought Will bitterly, where his heart would be if he had one.

"...and ... finally ... *that*," he wheezed, "is for dumb insolence ... to wit, failing ... to scream with ... agony and beg ... for mercy while ... being beaten."

Slowly, blinking tears from his eyes, Will stood up. He stared at Symon, who was leaning against the fireplace with a horrible gloating leer on his face. He turned to Doctor Blud. He took the bundle of rags out of his mouth. The very first time he had been beaten on Symon's behalf, he had nearly bitten through his tongue. Since then, he had used a bundle of rags to bite on to. This bundle was his fifth. He walked steadily across the room and dropped the rags into the wastebasket. He wouldn't be needing them any more.

Doctor Blud watched him with bleary, hate-filled eyes.

Will bowed to the schoolmaster. "Thank you, sir."

"Eh?" Doctor Blud jerked upright. "What the devil d'you mean, boy? Thank me, whelp? Thank me for what, I'd like to know?"

Will kept his voice level. "For my correction, sir."

The Doctor hissed through his teeth. "Defiance, insect? By the burning eyebrows of the Great Horned Beast of Bazak-Baroon, it's time you learnt respect for your betters! This is what comes of being schooled by Dame Fudge, is it? Has that foolish old baggage taught you nothing?"

"She taught me how to read and write," said Will. "And yes, she taught me to respect my betters, and so I do – when I meet them."

Symon didn't know whether to be outraged at Will's impertinence or delighted at the prospect of seeing him beaten again. He hopped from foot to foot. "Ooh, sir!" he gasped. "Did you hear that? He answered you back!"

Doctor Blud's unhealthy face turned purple with rage. "Dare to defy me, wretch, and by the Holy Nosehair of the Prophet Moo, I'll..."

"Beat me again?" Will gave a half-smile. "I believe you have done as much as you can in that way, sir." The schoolmaster's fists clenched. "But tomorrow is Symon's birthday. A Tournament will be held to honour his coming-of-age. Then he will be Lord Symon. He will no longer be taught by you and he will no longer need a whipping boy. He will go to Knyght School."

"He will, indeed."

Will spun round at the sound of the new voice behind him: a quiet, harsh voice, rumbling with not-quite-hidden menace.

Lord Gordin was standing by the door.

The High Lord of Dun Indewood had short, stumpy legs; but his muscular body and long arms seemed to belong to a much bigger man. His head and chin were covered with dark stubble. His skin was pockmarked and sallow. His eyes, deep-set and as dark as a beetle's back, peered between ragged eyebrows and a bristling moustache. He wore a pure white, woollen tunic with short sleeves to show off his many gold arm-rings. A golden torc made his thick neck look even shorter than it was. His belt buckle, the clasp that held his cloak, his earrings, were all of bright gold. Most people, on meeting the High Lord for the first time, thought him dangerous, coarse, ugly, stupid and brutal. They were wrong – Gordin wasn't stupid.

"Yes," said Lord Gordin. "Soon, my son will go to Knyght School." He reached forward and draped an arm, heavy with gold, round Symon's shoulders.

Will's mouth was dry. "And I shall follow him, my Lord," he said, "as you promised, many years ago."

"Indeed you shall." Lord Gordin's voice was soft. "You shall follow him. You may even carry his books, if you wish. And his armour. You may follow him as far as the gates."

Will gaped, unable to believe his ears.

The High Lord's eyes narrowed, reptile-like. "Yes, I promised you should follow Symon to Knyght School – not *into* Knyght School. I did not say you should become a pupil yourself."

CHAPTER FOUR

How the High Lord revealed himself to be a Low Worm and how Will became the Worm that Turned.

Will stared at Symon's smirk; Doctor Blud's leer; Lord Gordin's mirthless smile.

"You tricked me," he whispered.

"I?" Gordin looked puzzled. "Surely not."

Will felt rage bubbling up inside him. "You led me to believe I could go to…"

Gordin was no longer smiling. His voice rasped through the still air of the schoolroom. "What you believed does not matter. I never promised to send you to Knyght School. How dare you think yourself worthy? You are not the son of a gentleman."

A red mist seemed to float before Will's eyes.

"Don't feel so bad, Willum." Symon's mocking voice broke through Will's despair. "You can still go to the Poor School."

"Indeed," chimed in Doctor Blud. "A very full and valuable education for one of your station. While Symon is instructed in Grammarie, Physik and Mathematics, you will learn Humilitie…"

"Doing what you're told," cut in Symon.

"Servilitie…"

"Doing what you're told and looking pleased about it."

"…and Animal Husbandrie."

Symon thrust his fleshy face to within inches of Will's nose. "Feeding the pigs."

Will drew back one clenched fist.

Lord Gordin's voice cut through the air like a sword blade. "Touch my son and you are a dead man."

Slowly, Will lowered his fist. Turning, as if in a dream, he stumbled for the door.

"I have not dismissed you!" The High Lord's bark brought Will up short. "You will remain there until my son says you may go." And with a final glare, Gordin strode from the room.

Will, his face expressionless, turned and waited.

The High Lord's heir, the True Acorn of the Mighty Oak, completely ignored Will. He picked up a copy of *Big Men with Swords* and began to read it, or at least, to look at the pictures. Doctor Blud sat down in his chair and steepled his fingers watching Symon with approval.

After a few minutes, Will spoke up, "You wanted me to wait."

"Did I?" Symon pretended unconvincingly to rack his brains. "Oh, yes. I want you to be my squire in my coming-of-age Tournament."

Doctor Blud gave an approving cackle.

Will stared. "Your *what*?"

"It's a person who helps a Knyght to put on his armour and…"

"I know what a squire is," said Will tonelessly.

Symon shrugged. "Of course, you're normally the last person in the world I'd ask, but all my friends are actually in the Tournament, so it'll have to be some grovelling peasant – and at least you've had an education of sorts. Anyway I'm not *asking* you, I'm *ordering* you."

"I see," said Will. "That's all, is it?"

Symon waved a lordly hand in dismissal.

As Will walked stiffly down the corridor, he heard mocking laughter break out in the room behind him and echo throughout the castle. He hobbled painfully down the Longish Gallery feeling numb, in the way that someone who is hurt badly feels nothing before the pain begins.

His way led him through the Decaying Ballroom with its threadbare and faded tapestries. These had once shown scenes of glory and splendour, celebrating the brave deeds of the Kings of Dun Indewood. But the age of Kings was long gone. The castle's glorious past lay hidden beneath layers of dust and cobwebs.

He passed through the abandoned armoury, where peeling walls were lined with rusting weapons and the armour of long-dead Knyghts. Will had spent hours examining these with reverence, sighing for the days when the greatest Knyghts of the City – Sir Lunchalot the Well-Padded, Sir Cumspect the Cautious, Sir Insomnia the Sleepless – had ridden out on their adventures, perhaps in this very same armour.

Will reached the Underlings' Stair. There were many staircases in the castle but most of them were far too grand to be used by Will. You couldn't get more Underling than being Symon Mandrake's whipping boy, Will thought miserably. Even the castle cat was treated with more respect.

Will paused at the top of the dusty, gloomy steps – and then moved on, past the Bondsmen's Stair, the Butlers' Stair... on and on until he came to the Grand Stair. This, the most splendid of the castle's stairways, was for the use of the High Lord and his family only, and definitely off limits to Will. But today, he didn't care. Servants and guards stared in horrified amazement as he descended. He heard scandalised whispers, but no one tried to stop him, even when he carried on through the forbidden splendour of the Great Hall and the Ceremonial Doorway.

At the same unhurried pace, Will crossed the courtyard in the shadow of the ruined Citadel of the Kings. He passed the ivy-covered buildings of the Knyght School without a glance. Lost in a private world of misery and betrayal, Will went through the gatehouse and across the drawbridge, out of the castle.

He didn't notice a shadowy, hooded figure wrapped in a travel-stained robe, who stepped out from a corner of the gatehouse. Though bent with age, it moved swiftly and with purpose, following Will.

"Evenin', young Willum!" called out a voice from the guardhouse next to the City gates.

"Evening, Rolph." Will didn't trust his voice. He said nothing more, but stood and waited patiently for the guard to open the gate.

Rolph had a kind but rather stupid face. His rusty helmet was two sizes too big for him, and a badly dented breastplate didn't quite cover his spreading paunch. He jangled his keys and gave Will a slow smile. "A bit late tonight, Will." He caught Will's taut look. "Detained by our Lord Symon, was you?" Rolph shook his head knowingly. "What a pain in the bum, ey?"

Will rubbed his backside and nodded.

Rolph gestured vaguely towards the outside. "You'd better get out to the moor smartish. You don't want your pigs there at night. Not for anything."

Will nodded gravely, waved Rolph farewell and walked at the same even pace out of the gate, towards Four Heifer Moor where his father's pigs were foraging.

A clatter from a dark corner of the guardhouse distracted Rolph for a moment as he was shutting the gate. As the guard turned his head in the direction of the sound, the hooded figure slipped unseen through the half-closed gate.

The last rays of the sun were smouldering into darkness as Will herded the pigs into the hamlet of Swains Willingly. The tiny village looked like an untidy collection of mud and straw, which was exactly what it was. The villagers' shacks were thrown together out of whatever came to hand. In Swains Willingly, what mostly came to hand was straw, mud and cow muck. The village nestled against the City walls, like a frightened child clinging to its mother's skirt, flinching away from the threatening, limitless wilderness of the Dark Forest.

The inhabitants of Swains Willingly would much rather have lived in Dun Indewood, within the protection of its stout walls. But poor farmers could not afford to live in the City; in any case, the citizens needed food, and somebody had to grow it. The unfortunate peasants who lived in Swains Willingly eked out a meagre existence from the scrublands between the City and the Forest.

In their fields, oats, hedge fruits and root vegetables grew haphazardly and were harvested diligently. Those farmers that kept livestock took their beasts out on to the moors between the City walls and the sinister eaves of the Forest. At sunset, they brought them back to the safety of strong wooden pens. At times of special peril, the villagers were allowed to shelter within the City walls, as long as they could get inside before the panic-stricken citizens closed the gates. Swains Willingly was a different world from the castle; as different as chalk and cheese – or more accurately, as mud and marble.

"Late again!" Will's father, standing at the doorway of the small wattle shack that was home, glanced at the pigs. "Good job you brung them pigs home afore dark, or else…"

His mother bustled out. "Willum, where've you been? We've been worried, 'aven't we, Father?"

"Ay, we was, Mother." Will's father shooed the pigs towards a wooden pen. "What would 'ave happened if they pigs'd been left outside on the moor?"

Will's mother gave his father a reproving glance. "I meant as 'ow we was worried about our Willum."

Will's father grunted.

Without speaking, Will made his way past them and into the dark and smoky interior of the family hovel. He winced as he sat on the rough wooden bench next to the tiny fire.

"Did you have fun at the castle?" asked his mother.

Will shook his head. There was no point in expecting his parents to understand. They'd never wanted him to go to Knyght School anyway.

"Book larnin'!" Will's father would say. "What good did that ever do a body? Look at me! I never learnt to read nor write neither, and it's never done me no harm." Will would gaze at his father's sullen, mean, discontented face and say nothing. He couldn't really blame his father. All the inhabitants of Dun Indewood were trained from childhood to "Know Their Place".

Will, too, should have been brought up to understand that he would live and die a pig-keeper. But from his earliest childhood, a glorious promise had been held out to him – Knyght School! He would do what none of his family had ever done. He would become a Knyght of the City of Dun Indewood!

Will gazed at his supper of thin gruel – a sort of oatmeal soup that was usually tasty on a Sadday night, but was watered down all week "to make it go further". By Freeday it tasted like washing-up water. Tonight, Will couldn't face it. He left his bowl untouched, and went to bed.

As he lay on his thin, straw mattress, Will pulled a sheet of paper from his jerkin. It was creased and folded, and stained with his own fingermarks. It showed a picture of a Knyght on horseback. His face wore a noble, almost angelic look; his long hair streamed behind him. He held his sword as if he truly believed it could banish all the evil in the world.

There were words printed underneath the picture and Will read them for the thousandth time:

The glory of the fair City of Dun Indewood is its Knyghts; the Truest and Bravest men alive and the Flower of Chivalry.

A Knyght of Dun Indewood must uphold the Right and defend the Meek. He must be Just and Honourable in all his dealings. A strong man of his hands and Fearsome in battle, he must withal be Meek and Gentle in times of

*Peace. Only thus may he be worthy of his Vows; a True
and Perfect, Gentil Knyght.*

Will had torn the picture from one of Symon's books.
Symon never read them anyway, but Will did. He read
them every week while Doctor Blud was having his
afternoon nap, and Will was waiting to be beaten. He
knew every page by heart. This had been his dream for as
long as he could remember; to be a Knyght-Errant, and
wander through the Dark Forest, following glorious
Quests, having adventures and righting wrongs.

But now that dream was over – destroyed as though it
had never been.

Will got out of bed. He crumpled the picture in his
hands and threw it on the embers of the fire. He watched
as flames licked around the paper, reducing it to black
flakes that stirred fitfully in the draughts that whistled
through the ill-made walls. Then, stepping over his
father's snoring body, he lifted the latch of the hut and
went outside into the chill night air. A half moon shone
through wisps of cloud, casting a ghostly, silver-grey light
over the slumbering village.

Without hesitation, without a backward glance, Will
walked away from his home, away from the City, and into
the forbidding shadows of the Dark Forest. He had barely
reached the first trees when a shadow stepped out from
behind a blasted oak, barring his way.

"Hello, Will," said a familiar voice. "Bit late for a walk,
isn't it?"

It was Rose.

"What did I tell you about not coming into the Forest?" she said reproachfully. "You'd better get home before something nasty happens to you."

That was how the argument started. Far into the night, raised voices echoed among the trees as Rose insisted that Will should return home and Will steadfastly refused.

"I'm not going back," he insisted. "They have tricked me. They have betrayed me. Symon is even making me act as his squire in the Tournament tomorrow, just to rub it in."

"So you're running away." Rose's voice was scornful.

"Call it what you like."

"Oh, no you don't. You're going back," Rose told him. Her eyes glittered.

"Symon's not going to get the chance to crow over me. I'm leaving the City, and you can't stop me." Will stormed off.

Rose called after him, "I saved your life the other day. Didn't I?" Will stopped and gave a brief nod. "Then there is a debt of honour between us. Isn't that what a Knyght would say?"

"I'm not a Knyght," Will told her bitterly. "And I never will be."

"But you want to be."

Will nodded slowly.

"Then you should behave like one. I claim the debt."

Will's eyes glittered with fury. But he knew Rose was right. A Knyght must pay his debts. Rose was leaving him no choice.

"Go home. Go to the Tournament. Be Symon's squire."

Rose lowered her eyes. "Trust me, Will. It's important."

Will bit his lip. He gave Rose an angry nod, and turned away. He set off back to the village.

After he had gone, Rose said, "I didn't like doing that."

A hooded figure stepped out of the shadows. "You did what you had to."

Rose sighed. "I hope Will sees it that way."

"Sure he will," sneered a sarcastic voice from the bag on the old man's back. "Everyone enjoys a bit of moral blackmail now and then."

"Shut up," said Rose.

CHAPTER FIVE

How Will came to fight in the Great Tournament and what Progress he made therein.

The following day, Will strode across the jousting field, threading his way between the contestants' pavilions. Each one had the coat of arms of a noble family: the Duck Rampant of the deWormleys, the Chicken Courant of the fitzBadleys, the Lamb Bondant of the Beaupeeps. The Tournament field was dotted with these tents, each with a long, bright pennant snapping in the breeze.

Overlooking the lists, where the jousting competition would be held, a small wooden grandstand had been erected. That was for the noble families, who were still at breakfast. On the other side of the lists the people of Dun

Indewood had started to gather, and the vendors selling nuts, pies and mugs of ale were already busy.

Will had to report to the Master of Arms, who was in charge of scheduling the jousts. He found the official's tent, drew the flap back and entered.

"Hello there, young Will."

Sitting in the middle of the tent, surrounded by dozens of scrolls, sheets of parchment, quills and inkpots was Rolph, the gatekeeper.

"The Master's come down with a case of scrotty knee," explained Rolph in answer to Will's puzzled look. "So I've been lumbered with this job."

"He'll be all right, won't he?" Will was concerned. The Master of Arms was one of the few people at the castle who had shown Will any kindness. He allowed Will to exercise his horse in the sheep pasture, and had even given him a few jousting lessons when he thought nobody was looking.

"Oh, yurs," replied Rolph. "Scrotty knee never killed anyone. It's only dangerous if it spreads upwards and they've got him hanging upside down to make sure that doesn't happen. Ready for the Tournament, then?"

Will shrugged. "I suppose so."

Rolph looked around and lowered his voice. He'd heard about the High Lord's broken promise and didn't approve. "Look'ee here, Will," he said quietly, "you don't want to feel too bad about not goin' to Knyght School. I known young men of their hands, fighting men, grieve their hearts out to be one of them old Knyghts up at the castle. And what are they anyway? Just a bunch of old duffers who sit around all day drinkin' too much brandy and makin' up stories about wars they never been in an' dragons they never fought."

"That's not true!" said Will indignantly. "The Knyghts are true warriors, and the protectors and saviours of Dun Indewood."

Rolph gave Will a strange look. "If you say so, lad." He became businesslike. "Weigh-in at noon. Tell your man, no gouging, butting or jousting below the belt." Rolph grinned again and added in a hoarse whisper, "And I hope the little stinkbritches falls off his perishin' horse and breaks his nasty little neck."

Will grinned back, in spite of himself. The Tournament was a big occasion. All the new boys going to Knyght School were to fight each other for a Golden Lance. Symon's father would be expecting him to cover himself with glory. Savagely, Will hoped that Symon would fall off his horse into a pig-wallow and cover himself with something else entirely.

Come to think of it, Symon was a useless horseman and never took any exercise. The first time the Master at Arms had showed Symon how to hold a lance, he'd screamed, "Don't point that thing at me!" and run away to hide. He was bound to end up looking stupid. At least, Will thought, that would be a sight worth seeing.

Picking up Symon's saddle and Tournament number, Will went in search of the Dragon Flambant of the Mandrakes that would mark Symon's pavilion.

When Will entered Symon's tent, it seemed to be empty. Symon's gleaming armour was neatly laid out on racks and stools, but of Symon himself there was no sign. Will looked around. Where on earth could he have got to? Then he realised that the large chest in the middle of the floor seemed to be quivering.

Will flung back the lid. Symon was crouching inside the chest, trembling so hard that the stout wooden walls shook. He was quite obviously petrified with fear.

Will reached down and shook him. "What are you doing? The Tournament's about to start."

Symon gave a squeal of terror and tried to burrow deeper into the tunics and cloaks at the bottom of the box. Will grabbed Symon by the shoulder and hauled him up. "What's the matter with you?"

Symon stared at him, wild-eyed. "I can't go out there! I can't ride! I don't know how to fight!" His lip trembled. "I thought, when the time came, I'd just... be able to do it, you know? Because I'm nobly born and everyone knows that noblemen all know how to fight. But there'll be people out there in armour with beastly great long spears trying to kill me!"

Will shook his head impatiently. "The spears are all blunt..."

Symon rolled his eyes in terror. "Blunt!"

"...and the armour's padded..."

"Padded!" Symon looked as if he was about to faint.

"Yes, for when you fall off your horse. It won't hurt much," said Will. He wrestled briefly with his conscience, and lost. "It'll hurt a lot," he added maliciously.

"Fall off my…" Symon went limp. Will shook him again.

"Leave me alone!" Symon swatted at Will's hands. "It's all your fault! If I hadn't bunked off all those jousting practices to get you into trouble, I'd know how to do all this Tournament stuff…" Will was speechless. "And now I'm supposed to go out and fight people when I don't know how. Well, I won't do it, d'you hear?"

"You've got to," Will told him. "You're the High Lord's son. What will people think if you don't fight?"

A cunning glint crept into Symon's piggy eyes. "They wouldn't have to know." He grabbed Will's sleeve. "As long as someone wearing my armour goes into the lists, everyone'll think it's me."

"Oh, no…" Will backed away.

"I'll give you anything!" Symon's frightened face took on a cunning leer. "I'll see you get to Knyght School – I'll talk to my father – I'll make him send you."

"I don't believe you." Will gazed at Symon with contempt. But there was no conviction in his voice. He couldn't trust Symon, but if he took Symon's place in the Tournament, surely Symon wouldn't dare go back on his word? "We'd never get away with it," he said uncertainly.

Symon brushed that aside. "Why not? We're the same size, and with the visor down no one will see your face."

"Well…"

"Good man! I knew you'd do it!" Symon dived for the back of the tent and began wriggling his way out.

Will stared at his wobbling bottom.

"Just a minute! How am I supposed to arm myself?"

"You'll think of something." Symon's voice was muffled. With a jerk, his legs shot out of sight. After a moment, he stuck his head back under the tent and hissed, "If anyone wants me, I'll be cowering under my bed." Then he disappeared.

"Oh, dearie, dearie me."

Will spun on his heel and stared at the figure lounging just inside the tent flap. A boy of about his own age – or was it? Surely it couldn't be…

"*Rose?*"

Rose had arranged her hair in a regulation page-boy cut and was wearing a squire's tunic. She grinned at Will. "It looks to me as if we have a situation here. So, Symon cut out and left you to fight for him." Rose picked up Symon's mail shirt. "Time to put your armour on, Sir Knyght."

Will stepped back in alarm. "I can't have you dressing me!"

"Why not?"

"Because… because…" Will drew a deep breath and tried his last line of defence. "Because girls aren't allowed to be squires."

"Well, pig boys aren't allowed to be Knyghts."

Will felt his face turn red. "Oh, well, when you put it that way…"

As she dropped the mail shirt over Will's head, Rose turned towards the tent flap and winked. A hooded figure outside gave a single nod, and moved away.

Ten minutes later, feeling slightly dazed, Will was standing by the lists watching the first joust. The Marshal of the Lists strode out into the middle of the field and raised his arms for silence.

"People of Dun Indewood!" he roared. "My lordz, ladeez 'n' gennlemun, yeomen, yeowomen, serfs and villeins; introducing a heavyweight armourplate contest, one fall, one submission or a violent death to decide the winner… between, in the blue corner, Norm dePlume…" (ironic cheers from the crowd) "…and, in the red corner, Tomus Beaupeep." (Boos and catcalls.) "Squires away, joust one!"

Now the Tournament was beginning, Will could hardly contain his excitement. He was actually going to joust. And, thanks to this armour, nobody would recognise him!

There were cheers and groans from the crowd as a lucky blow from Norm sent Tomus spinning out of his saddle. The first joust was over. Will glanced around. "It'll be my turn in a minute," he said aloud.

"There's no rush," said Rose, appearing at his side. "You're in the second half of the draw." She pointed at one of the new competitors cantering away to the opposite end of the field. "Watch out for your friend Jervaise deLacey." She grimaced. "He's a nasty piece of work."

Will watched as the hulking deLacey disposed of his opponent in double quick time, and nodded. "He always was a bad-tempered brute."

Rose grinned. "I daresay you'd be bad-tempered if you had a name like Jervaise deLacey."

At last, it was Will's turn to mount up. He stood on a sort of platform while his horse was brought up to stand alongside it. The horse was a destrier, a warhorse; it was wearing armour on its head, its chest and its haunches, with a sort of brightly coloured coat over the rest of its body that looked like a long tablecloth. Will scrambled into the saddle and Rose handed him his lance.

"This is crazy!" Will hissed. "I don't know how to do this!"

"Well, I'm no expert," Rose told him, "but I think you're supposed to prod your opponent with this pole until he falls off his horse."

"It's not a pole. It's a lance."

"Whatever. Prod away. Enjoy yourself."

The lance was a spear made of ash, over four yards long and very heavy. Will carried it in his right hand and his shield in his left. Trying to hold the reins, the lance and the shield with only two hands was quite a feat of juggling, but the horse seemed to know what it was doing. It automatically trotted to its starting position at the end of the lists, and Will didn't try to interfere.

His opponent, Nygel deWormley, had already reached the opposite end of the enclosure. Will's horse pawed at the ground as the Marshal raised his arm, and let a handkerchief fall from his hand. As it touched the ground, Nygel spurred his horse forward. Will's horse needed no urging and broke into a lumbering trot, which grew faster and faster until they were pounding along in a full charge.

Will found that he was fully occupied with trying not

to fall off or be shaken to bits inside his armour. At the same time, he was trying desperately to hold his lance steady and point it at Nygel.

As they came together, Will saw with relief that Nygel's lance point was wavering about all over the place. The bad news was that his own lance was also going to miss Nygel by miles. So he was more than a little surprised to see Nygel fly backwards off his horse and land on the ground with a noise like an explosion in a blacksmith's forge.

There was some polite applause, mostly from the people around Lord Gordin. Will stared blankly at his lance. Was it some kind of magical weapon that threw opponents down even when it didn't actually touch them?

As he trotted back to the mounting block, Will noticed a hooded figure standing with Rose, apparently deep in conversation. The stranger moved away at Will's approach.

"Wasn't that the traveller I saw in your cottage?" he asked, flinging his reins to Rose and sliding off the horse with an undignified wobble.

Rose nodded. "He seems to be staying in the City these days." She took Will's lance. "Nice work – for a beginner."

"I don't understand it." Will shrugged, not an easy thing to do in armour. "I never touched him."

"Fancy that," Rose said with a grin.

"Well, I didn't!"

"You're too modest." Rose gave Will a comradely smack across the shoulders that made him stagger. "Only a few bouts to go and you'll be in the final. Go get 'em, champ!"

CHAPTER SIX

Yet more of the Same Tournament and how it ended.

The next couple of hours were like a dream. Part of Will's mind (the part that was always reminding him to wash his hands before meals) knew that all he was doing, really, was managing not to fall off his horse; but as he continued to win jousts with ridiculous ease, his confidence soared. On his next tilt, the point of his lance caught Alin Sans Pitie with the force of a blow from a moth's wing; but Alin catapulted out of his saddle as if a battering ram had hit him.

The sullen silence of the crowd might have told Will what was really going on, but he just put it down to Symon's unpopularity. It wasn't until Jems fitzBadly tumbled off his horse a couple of seconds *after* he and Will had passed, with neither striking the other, that Will smelled a rat. He was seething as he handed his lance back to Rose.

"It's a fix!" he snapped. "They've all been told that Symon's got to win, so they're falling off on purpose."

Rose sniffed. "You don't say."

Will gave her a hard stare (a waste of time as the visor was in the way). "You knew!"

Rose gave him a pitying glance. "It doesn't take a genius to work it out. You'd have to be a fool to beat the High Lord's son at his own coming-of-age Tournament."

"But it's not fair!" protested Will. "They're not trying."

"Just as well," said Rose brutally. "You wouldn't have lasted long if they had been."

Too annoyed to reply, Will turned to watch the next bout just as Jervaise deLacey sent his latest rival spinning from his horse and into the mud. Jervaise certainly wasn't jousting to lose.

Will seethed in impotent rage. "It's not right," he protested. "It's not chivalrous."

Rose shook her head. "It's real life," she said. "Not something out of a story book."

"I don't care," said Will. "I'm not going through with this farce. I'm going to tell them who I am."

Rose raised an eyebrow. "Lord Gordin isn't going to be very impressed, is he?" She ticked off points on her fingers. "Impersonating the True Heir, Entering a Tournament Without Due Care and Attention, Wearing

Armour With Intent to Cause a Breach of the Peace and Being Poor in Charge of a Horse. You've already broken enough laws to be locked in the deepest dungeon and have the key melted down for hairpins."

There was a pause as Will considered this.

"In that case, I'll make sure I lose!" he cried. "I'll simply do what they're all doing; just fall off my horse."

"And they'll fall off their horses at the same time and you'll have to have a rematch," countered Rose. "You can't both keep falling off your horses all day."

"All right!" Will wailed. "So what do I do?"

"You've got this far, so you might as well try and win."

"I'm not going to have to try very hard, am I?" replied Will bitterly.

In the semi-final, Will was drawn against Rojah leGross; a heavyweight contender who had come through the earlier rounds simply because no one had strength enough to knock him off his horse. On the first pass, Rojah had clearly been struggling to fall off, but as he was pretty well wedged in the saddle, this was impossible. On the second run, Will actually managed to break his spear on his opponent (there was quite a lot of Rojah to hit), but to Will's disappointment, it had no effect.

Will rode back to his tent for another lance. As she passed him the replacement, Rose leapt up on to Will's stirrup and hissed in his ear: "Don't bother with your lance – use your shield – knock his spear point into the ground."

Will nodded and rode back in readiness for the third tilt.

As he thundered towards his opponent, Will twisted in his saddle and thrust his shield out and downwards. The point of Rojah's lance slid across it and dipped until its point stuck firmly in the turf. The lance suddenly became a vaulting pole. Rojah flew out of his saddle and soared high over the jousting field in a graceful arc. This ended in a wet "splat" as Rojah stuck head first in a mudhole with his legs waving in the air. It took three men to dig him out.

Will was through to the Final.

Rose gave Will a drink through a straw so he wouldn't have to take his visor off. "Now, listen," she said urgently. "You're up against a big boy this time. I told you to watch Jervaise deLacey. Nobody's laid a spear on him yet. And he fights dirty. Watch yourself."

Will shook his head. "What does it matter?" he said wretchedly. "He'll fall off like the rest of them."

Rose patted him on the shoulder. "Don't worry about it. Maybe he'll smash you into a bloody pulp instead."

"Thanks for the encouragement." Will took his spear from her, and cantered to the end of the field. He turned to face Jervaise. The Marshal of the Lists dropped his handkerchief, and they were off.

On the first pass, Jervaise charged towards Will with his lance pointing unwaveringly at Will's chest. At the last moment, he flicked the point aside contemptuously, allowing Will to gallop on untouched.

On the second tilt, he did the same thing; but Will, whose lance had been wavering about even more than usual, almost dropped the spear altogether. He made a frantic grab to recover it, accidentally bringing the point up to deliver a crashing blow to Jervaise's helmet.

That did it. Jervaise had never been happy about following his father's orders and losing to Symon, and the blow on his head made him lose his temper completely. On the third tilt, he came towards Will as if he'd decided to impale him on his lance like a butterfly on a pin. Will's horse, more battle-wise than his master, saw the danger and side-stepped nimbly at the last moment. This had the incidental effect of bringing Will's wildly swinging lance straight into Jervaise's shield, which shattered.

Will snatched another lance from Rose. "That's more like it! He wants to fight now."

Rose looked worried. "Watch him, Will," she called. "He'll try something dirty this time!"

Jervaise was shaken. He was a violent bully, but he also had a very firm belief in self-preservation. He began to think he'd underestimated his opponent. He was still angry and determined to win – but on his own terms. He and Will galloped towards each other for the third time.

Will held his lance steady, aiming for Jervaise's shield. But at the last moment, Jervaise brought his lance sweeping down. Will shot from the saddle as Jervaise's spear became entangled in his horse's legs and it went down with a scream of agony. The crowd leapt up shouting "Foul!"

Will staggered to his feet in a daze, and ran to help his horse, which was thrashing about, struggling to get to its feet.

"Look out!" Will heard Rose's shrill cry above all the clamour of the crowd. Instinctively, he ducked, just as Jervaise's sword whistled through the air in an attempt to lop his head clean off his shoulders.

Rage boiled in Will. He snatched up his lance, which he had dropped when he fell. He stood in a crouch and waited as Jervaise spun his charger round and came back, sword raised for another blow.

But as the sword swung, Will swayed to one side and brought the lance sweeping around in a scything blow. He might not know much about jousting, but he had been defending his pigs with a quarterstaff against attacks from wolves and bears for as long as he could remember. His roundhouse swipe sent Jervaise tumbling from his saddle, his sword spinning away.

Will drew his own sword and raced towards the struggling figure. He put the point of the sword into the gap between the helmet and mail jacket, and gripped the handle with both hands.

"Yield," he said grimly.

"I yield! I yield!"

Will stepped back, shaking with anger and shock. The Tournament was over. He had won! He saw that Rose was already helping his trembling horse to its feet. Two men-at-arms stepped forward to escort him to the grandstand, while the crowd gave a very half-hearted round of applause.

Gordin stood up and gave him a ferocious smile. Will's blood ran cold. He'd never thought about what would happen if he won the Tournament.

"You have done well, my son." Gordin took the golden lance that was the prize for the Tournament. "Doff your helm and receive your prize."

Will glanced frantically from side to side. But Gordin was waiting, and starting to frown now. Shaking, Will reached up and unlaced his helm. He drew it off and raised his head. There was a collective gasp from the nobles around Gordin.

The High Lord gave a bellow of rage. "What is this?"

Someone in the crowd called out, "Hey, that's not Symon – that's Edwid the Swineherd's lad. Three cheers for Willum!"

The crowd burst into wild applause mixed with hoots of delighted laughter. Gordin looked as if he was about to burst a blood vessel. His face turned red. His muscles knotted. The nearer members of the crowd shifted back uneasily. The applause and laughter died.

"You have impersonated my son. You have falsely claimed the right to a trial of arms with men of noble birth!" The crowd was silent now. Gordin drew his sword and pointed it at Will. "Take this miscreant away and hang him from the highest tower in the castle!"

Will stood transfixed with shock.

Two burly guards moved forward. As they closed in on Will, a tall figure in a cloak stepped out from the crowd. "My Lord! Thou art mistaken!"

Gordin turned his anger on the newcomer. "Who are you, to question the High Lord of the City?"

The man pulled back his hood. "Think back, my Lord. Thou knowest who I am."

"Take a good look," said a sneering voice that seemed to come from the bag strapped to the stranger's back. "Ring any bells? Six-three, skinny as a broomstick, white hair, hooked nose, piercing grey eyes? Probably a bit wrinklier than you remember…" The stranger jabbed the bag with his elbow and the voice died away to resentful mutterings.

Gordin lowered his sword. It was impossible for a man of his complexion to turn pale, but his face became an unhealthy colour.

The man in the cloak gave a slight bow. "My Lord, I am in the happy position of being able to put right a misunderstanding. I happened to be present when thy son committed an act of great generosity."

"Hah!" The voice from the bag across the old man's shoulders was scornful, but very, very quiet.

Will gaped at the stranger. Surely nobody who knew Symon would believe for a moment that he had ever committed a generous act of any kind, let alone a great one? But Gordin stared at the speaker as a bird might stare at a snake. "Go on," he said in a hoarse whisper.

"Knowing how much his friend wished to prove his

66

valour to thee," the speaker went on smoothly, "thy son, though he would have given the world to fight in the Tournament, selflessly allowed his name and his armour to be used by his friend Will."

"That's the most ridiculous story I've ever heard!" said the voice from the bag, in shocked tones. "And when it comes to ridiculous stories, believe me, I'm an expert." The tall man jerked his elbow again and the muffled voice was stilled.

"It was Symon's most earnest wish," the stranger continued, "that, by this proof of his courage, his dearest friend should be allowed to join him at Knyght School. My Lord, wilt thou allow his sacrifice to have been made in vain?"

Lord Gordin almost choked with fury. He knew the old man's story was preposterous, but he couldn't say so without admitting that his son was not only ungenerous, but a coward. "A swineherd cannot go to Knyght School!" he snapped.

"But Squire Willum deSanglier could," the old man countered quickly.

Gordin looked as if he was chewing beetles, but he nodded slowly. He fixed Will with a glare of pure malice.

"Very well," he rasped. He raised his left hand, palm outwards. "Be it known that this day, Willum of the House of deSanglier is hereby admitted to Knyght School..."

The rest of his speech went unheard as the crowd erupted into wild cheering. The man in the cloak watched impassively as Rose slapped Will on the back, while he stood in a daze with tears of joy running down his cheeks.

CHAPTER SEVEN

How Will became a pupil at the Knyght School and how Mad Dog Reggie sent Filip le Cul-de-Sac on a Perilous Quest.

"Who was he?" Will looked earnestly at Rose, who said nothing. "You must know. He *was* the man in your cottage, wasn't he?"

Rose shrugged. "When he wants you to know, he'll tell you."

"Gordin was afraid of him," mused Will, "that's for sure."

It was almost sunset on the day of the Tournament. Will and Rose were sitting on a log where the sheep-pasture melted into the Forest. Will was chewing moodily on a grass stalk. He had wanted to thank the man in the cloak, but immediately after the Tournament the stranger had vanished. Rose, who clearly knew who the old man was, wouldn't tell Will anything.

"So, you're going to live at the Knyght School," said Rose. "Do your parents mind?"

"Not really," said Will. "My mother wasn't too keen at first, but my father was happy enough. He just said, 'More food for the pigs'."

Rose looked at Will slantwise. "What's all this 'deSanglier' stuff anyway?" she asked.

"Oh, that!" Will shrugged dismissively. "Sanglier means 'wild boar' in the Old Language. I read it in one of Symon's books. So it's a grand way of saying 'Will the pig boy'. I suppose they think if they give me an aristocratic sounding name, they needn't be ashamed to send their kids to school with me," he went on bitterly.

Rose sniffed. "Some people are never satisfied."

"I don't mean... it's not that... it's just... oh, I don't know." Will irritably threw the grass stalk away. He suddenly felt awkward. "Anyway, I have to go now. Thanks for being my squire... and... er... everything." Hesitantly, he held out his hand. Grinning, Rose shook it.

"Are you sure you want to go to Knyght School?" she asked as Will felt his fingers to make sure Rose's grip hadn't broken any. "We could use you in the Forest."

Will wasn't a pompous person, but he felt too strongly about this subject to speak naturally and took refuge in one of the phrases he had learnt from Symon's book. "I must go to Knyght School. It is the desire of my heart."

Rose tossed her head. "Well, la-di-dah. See you around, Sir Knyght."

Will groaned. "No, wait. I didn't mean..."

But Rose had already melted into the shadows of the Dark Forest.

The next morning, Will left home early. He called in at the tiny village school to say goodbye to old Dame Fudge, who cried over him. Then he set off for the City, entering it as soon as the gates were opened.

"'Ullo, Will!" Rolph called as he went in. "Back on duty. By the by, you was great in the Tournament. Showed 'em all!"

Will waved to Rolph and walked on through the narrow, twisting streets, climbing all the time, until he arrived at the gatehouse of the castle. Lord Gordin's guards let him in through the wicket gate and sent him to join a group of skylarking boys of his own age. One of them was Jervaise deLacey, who immediately fixed Will with a look of utter hatred. The others, taking their cue from Jervaise, turned their noses up or stared at his thin, patched clothing. Will ignored them and pretended to look around him as if he'd never seen the familiar buildings of the castle before.

Across the courtyard, perched on the highest point of the hill of Bel Mont, loomed the Citadel of the Kings. The citadel was a ruin. It had not been used since the death of the last King, and now stood empty, silent and brooding. Since he had first come to the castle, the citadel had fascinated Will. He longed to explore the ancient fastness, but its doorways were barred. Only ravens peered from its empty windows and flapped, screeching, through its dark chambers.

Below the citadel, the rest of the castle was built in a rough rectangle around the courtyard where Will now stood. One of the longer sides held the High Lord's apartments, the council chambers, and the living quarters of the Knyghts. On the opposite side stood the Knyght School. On either side of the gatehouse lived Lord Gordin's guards and the ragged servants who kept the castle more or less running.

The castle had an unplanned look. Walls, towers and turrets reared here and there, higgledy-piggledy. Over the years, bits had collapsed and been replaced with new bits that must have seemed like a good idea at the time. There were round towers, square towers, towers with any number of sides from three to eight. Some had long, thin, pointy windows, some had short, fat, dumpy ones. Large chambers sat on top of smaller ones, which groaned and buckled under their weight.

At length, a senior boy gathered the new pupils and took them into the Knyght School to find their dormitories.

"Choose your own beds," he announced. "Put your belongings in your lockers and report for assembly in one hour. Oh, and don't forget, armour inspection tomorrow after breakfast."

Under cover of the chatter, Will approached the senior boy. "Please, sir…"

"I'm merely a student like yourself," drawled the senior boy. "You don't have to 'sir' me." He looked at Will for the first time and wrinkled his nose. "On the other hand, perhaps you do."

"I haven't got any armour," Will blurted out.

"Why not? Every new boy was sent a list of what to bring on the first day…"

"I only found out I was coming to Knyght School yesterday," protested Will.

"That's not my fault. You'll have to find some armour or be expelled."

Will groaned inwardly. He was penniless. How could he possibly get hold of a suit of armour for inspection the following morning? Unless…

Will had no belongings to put in his locker anyway. He left the other boys unpacking and raced across the courtyard to the other side of the castle, heading for the abandoned armoury…

"Oh dear, oh dear, oh dear."

The armourer pursed his lips. He reached across the counter and turned a rusty breastplate over. He sucked air through his teeth. He shook his head.

"Well?" said Will anxiously. "Can you fix it?"

The armourer gave Will an indignant look. "Fix it? I daren't even *touch* some of it, squire. It's only the rust that's holding it together. You'll never get it through its MOT."

"MOT?"

"Ministry of Tournaments. They test everyone's armour to make sure it'll stand up to a blow from a lance. This lot wouldn't stand up to a flick from a wet towel." He held up a pair of corroded steel shin-pads. "Your greaves are a total write-off, see, squire – and as for your pauldrons – oh dear, oh dear, oh dear."

"But it's all I've got," protested Will. "I thought you could let it out a bit…"

"Let it out a bit?" The armourer closed his eyes.

"…and with a bit of welding…"

"A bit of welding?" The armourer laughed bitterly. "There's nothing left to weld! I'll melt it down for you if you like. There's probably enough sound metal in there to make you a nice belt-buckle."

Will felt tears stinging his eyes. "Please – couldn't you try? It's all I have."

The armourer sighed gustily. "All right, all right. Leave it with me… I'll see what I can do."

"Thank you!" Will was overjoyed. "I'll pick it up tomorrow morning, first thing."

"Tomorrow morn…?" The armourer gazed at the armour that had once belonged to Sir Cularsaw the Violent and shook his head in disbelief.

"It'll cost yer, mind!" he called after Will who was

shooting up the stairs. He was already late for assembly.

At about the same time, the drudge who was supposed to keep the armoury tidy stood in front of an armour-shaped darker patch on the sun-bleached wall and scratched his head. "That's funny," he muttered to himself. "I could have sworn it was there yesterday..."

As luck would have it – at least, the sort of luck that always happened to *him*, Will thought bitterly – he burst into the School Hall the moment after everyone had sat down, following the entrance of the Head and his staff.

The Head threw him a venomous look. "You, boy! Come here!"

With an inward groan, and trying to keep his legs steady, Will walked down between the long rows of boys. At every step he heard stifled sniggers and whispered remarks which, he was sure, were not meant kindly.

As he approached them, Will weighed up the staff of the Knyght School. They were not, he thought, a very impressive lot. There was Symon's former tutor, Doctor Blud, maliciously delighted that Will was in trouble so soon; and his predecessor, Professor Bone, who looked as if he belonged in a tomb but had been given the day off. As for the rest, the ones who didn't look crushed and apprehensive looked half-asleep.

Will halted before the Head of the Knyght School, Sir Regynild le Bêtenoire (known to the pupils as Mad Dog Reggie). The Head had a birds'-nest beard and bloodshot eyes and was, at the moment, going purple in the face.

"What d'ye mean," he thundered, "dam' ye, sir, what d'ye mean by bursting inter me school like a bally bull in a bally potter's workshop? Eh? What d'yer mean by it?"

Will gulped. "Please, sir..."

"Don't answer back! Blud, Blud!" Will thought for a moment the Head was ordering his execution, until he saw Doctor Blud step forward. "What boy is this? What's the bally blatherskite doin' here, eh? Eh?"

Doctor Blud bowed. You could have fried eggs in his voice. "This is the new boy, so please your worship."

Sir Regynild's eyes practically popped out of his head. "New boy?" He gave Will's shabby tunic an appalled and disbelieving glance. "D'yer mean to tell me that this blasted blowfly, this blithering blob of bloat, is supposed to be a pupil in this school?! Dear heaven!" The Head dragged a hip-flask from under his threadbare academic gown. He took a generous swig and went into a coughing fit. When he could speak again, he leaned down and barked, "What's yer beastly bally name, you bloodstained bludger of a boy?"

"Willum the Swine..." Will stopped. There was an outburst of giggles from behind him. "Willum of the House of deSanglier, if you please, sir."

Sir Regynild bent down lower. His foul breath flowed over Will, and drops of spittle struck his face. "Listen to me, you foul fermentation of festering filth," he spat, "you loathsome lickspittle lobworm! Lord Gordin may do what he will, but any whining whelp he sends to me will learn to still its bally bark and stay in its kennel, mark me now! Or I'll have its greasy, grizzly guts for galligaskins!"

Every boy in the school was staring as Will bowed to the Head and went back down the hall to a vacant place. Most of the boys were grinning at Will's discomfiture (Will noticed Symon saying something to his neighbour that sent them both into silent hysterics), but a few looked sympathetic. Will squeezed on to a bench beside a solid, cheerful-looking youngster with a dense mop of black curls, who seemed to have spread most of his breakfast over the front of his tunic.

At a signal from Sir Regynild, the assembly began to groan its way through a tuneless ballad:

> *In days of old*
> *When Knyghts were bold*
> *And also brave and dashing,*
> *They'd seek out dragons and their ilk*
> *And give them such a bashing.*
>
> *Some sought in vain*
> *And some were slain,*
> *And all had cause to rue it.*
> *Sing tra-la-lee, and pray that we*
> *Will never have to do it.*

Will didn't think the words sounded very noble. He was quite relieved when the song ended and Sir Regynild stood up.

"Today," he growled, "as is customary on the first day of term, the three most senior boys are ready to graduate from the Knyght School." There were murmurs and a smattering of applause. "It therefore falls to me to set each candidate a Quest, from which he will emerge with glory and renown as a full Knyght of the City of Dun Indewood – or perish horribly in the attempt!"

The pupils around Will cheered and clapped wildly. Will felt a thrill course through his veins. This was more like it! A Quest! Knyght-Errantry!

"Filip le Cul-de-Sac," bellowed the Head, nodding to a dough-faced senior boy who stood up, looking apprehensive. "Thy task, with which to try thy mettle and prove thy manhood, shall be..." He paused impressively as Will held his breath, his heart pounding. What fantastically dangerous and amazingly foolhardy task would this brave squire be set to prove himself a worthy Knyght of Dun Indewood?

"Thy task shall be," repeated the Head in ringing tones, "...to bring unto me an egg from the hen of Mistress Scroffly!"

Chapter Eight

How Will rescued a Pastafarian and
became a Delivery Boy for Luigi's Pizzas
(Fast Service or Your Money Back).

Will could hardly believe his ears. He watched in disbelief as Filip turned pale and staggered. The curly-haired boy to his right drew in his breath sharply and tutted under his breath. Will leaned towards him and whispered, "He can't be serious!"

The boy shook his head. "Poor Filip. He will be hard-pressed." He turned a wide-eyed gaze to Will. "I know that chicken. It's really *vicious*!"

Will's jaw dropped, but Sir Regynild was speaking again, sending Bryun le Chien Méchant on a Quest to Mistress Soape the Washerwoman to collect his clean tights, while

Mal deMer was to go to the market and pick up some nice soft hankies. The whole school prayed for the candidates' success and safe return, and the assembly was over.

The curly-haired boy gave Will a friendly grin. "You're in my form," he said. "I'm Gyles le Cure Hardy." He held out his hand. Gratefully, Will shook it.

"What was all that about?" he asked as he and Gyles pushed their way through a corridor full of skylarking boys in the blue-and-red striped surcoats of the Knyght School. "I thought when a squire went on a Quest to become a Knyght he had to do something really brave and daring, like fighting an ogre or slaying a dragon."

Gyles looked a bit downcast. "Well, yes," he said, "they used to do that sort of thing once; but then parents started complaining that the Forest had grown too dangerous. So many boys were excused fighting dragons, the whole thing had to be rethought. So now all they do is send you on a – well, an errand really, and call it a Quest."

Will felt his whole world beginning to crumble about his ears. "So nobody gets sent on Quests into the Forest any more?"

"No. Some of the senior boys ride in a little way – just for swank you know – they call it…"

"Going for a spin in the woods, I know." Will remembered the Highwaywolf. "But what about the teachers? What about the Knyghts who live in Knyghts Gogently? Don't they ever go into the Forest?"

"What for?" Gyles seemed genuinely puzzled. "It's dangerous."

Will felt like saying that was the whole point; but after all, it was his first day at school and Gyles was the only person who had shown any signs of wanting to be friendly. Will didn't want to upset him. Another thought struck him. "What are galligaskins?"

Gyles wrinkled his brow. "A sort of leather trousers, I think. The trouble is," he went on as they reached their classroom, "the Forest is too big. A hundred Knyghts could spend a hundred years out there and never tame a quarter of it. And there's nowhere to go."

"But aren't there other cities, like ours?" asked Will. "I read that..."

Gyles shrugged. "That's what the legends say," he agreed, "but nobody knows where they are, if they're still there, or whether they ever really existed at all. So why go looking? It's much safer to stay at home."

As the weeks wore on, Will became even more disenchanted with Knyght School. All the other boys were the children of rich and powerful parents. They didn't have to work hard to get what they wanted, because they generally got it anyway without doing any work at all. Most of them were vain and stupid. They weren't clever or energetic enough to be good at bullying (except for a few like Symon, who really worked at it), but they felt threatened by poor people who asked too many questions and *didn't know their place.* As Will was clearly such a person, many of his schoolmates did their half-hearted best to be unpleasant to him. They left him out of things and made nasty comments about his parents, his upbringing and his clothes.

Gyles had lent Will his spare surcoat, so at least he had the proper uniform. But Will's armour, when it came back from the armourer's workshop, looked like a patchwork quilt; and, no matter how hard he tried, he could never polish all the rust stains out of it.

What really upset Will was the lack of interest his fellow pupils – and, come to that, the teachers – showed in their classes. Hardly any of the boys took the riding lessons and weaponry instruction seriously. Symon never did them at all and many of the other boys had dog-eared notes that they brought out whenever they thought they could get away with it.

The other lessons weren't much better. Will learnt how to use an astrolabe, which was an instrument that could tell you where you were by the positions of the stars; but since nobody from Dun Indewood ever went anywhere, they always knew where they were anyway. Poetry and Musik were limited because there wasn't much in the way of brave deeds to sing or write about.

"What's the point of all this stuff?" Gyles asked one day, slamming his book shut in disgust. "I mean why do we have to learn the Theory of Falconry? Nobody in the castle has kept a falcon for ages!"

"Only because nobody can be bothered to catch a

hawk and train it properly," said Will mildly.

"Exactly! And as for Venery – well," Gyles went on more quietly, looking rather shamefaced, "hunting, you know. Nobody does that sort of thing any more."

Nevertheless, Will continued to take all his studies seriously, hoping that all the knowledge that nobody seemed to need or want any more would come in handy some day.

There were compensations. Now that Will was living at the Knyght School, he had plenty of opportunities to explore the castle. He spent what free time he had wandering through its forgotten, dusty rooms and corridors.

This was how he discovered the Corridor of Lost Kings, whose dark walls were covered with gloomy pictures of sad-looking men wearing crowns and hangdog expressions. He visited the Chamber of Wise Counsellors, thick with dust, and the Hall of Shining Treasures which was completely empty. All the treasures, shining or otherwise, which the Knyghts of Dun Indewood had brought back from their Quests, had gone missing years ago and never been replaced.

Another good reason for exploring the castle was that it kept Will out of Symon's way. Symon's father had not been amused at the deception practised on him at the Tournament and had evidently made Symon suffer for his cowardice and falsehood. Symon, naturally, blamed Will for his misfortune.

But Symon wasn't interested in the history and legends of the castle. As far as he was concerned, its crumbling rooms held no secrets and nothing worth stealing. He spent most of his time lazing about in his own rooms (he had seventeen all to himself), eating and drinking things that were bad for his teeth, his skin and his disposition, and thinking up wicked schemes. These mostly had to do with tormenting small animals (which couldn't fight back) and servants (who daren't).

One of the few things that could rouse Symon from his usual state of lethargy was the daily pizza delivery. The pizzas were made by Luigi the Pastafarian, who sold pasta and pizza from his *Fasta Pasta on the Piazza* restaurant in the Beau Monde district, and operated a delivery service. He did a roaring trade.

The boys from the Knyght School were not supposed to order pizzas. They were supposed to eat what the Knyght School cook called "nourishing, wholesome food", and the pupils referred to as "revolting slop". The food didn't bother Will; it was much better than what he was used to at home.

However, the rule against ordering pizza didn't seem to apply to Symon. So when Will heard what sounded like a wild bull charging past the door of his dormitory one evening, he glanced out of the window. Sure enough, Luigi the Pastafarian was just pulling up in the courtyard, his rainbow-coloured dreadlocks bobbing cheerfully as he got down from his dogcart.

Symon never seemed to know when lessons were supposed to start, but he always knew to the minute when the pizza delivery was due to arrive. Symon appeared at the courtyard door, licking his lips ravenously. He crossed to the cart and bore his pizza off in triumph.

Also hanging around the courtyard were several boys. Their yapping cries, floating up to Will's open window, clearly showed that they had fewer manners than brains. Will looked out again. The boys were now surrounding Luigi.

"Hey, fatso! Who's been eating all the pasta?"

"I say, mophead! Got any tootsie frootsie ice cream?"

The pastafarian busied himself assembling a pile of pizza boxes from his dogcart. "Now then, boys. You've had your fun, s'pose you just let me get on with my job, peaceful-like." He lifted the tottering pile of boxes and turned towards the main door to the Knyght School.

As he stepped forward, a foot shot out. Will gave an angry yell as, with a cry of "Holy cannelloni!", the pastafarian tripped. Pizza boxes flew in all directions and Luigi fell, fetching his head a nasty crack against a stone pillar. Laughing, his tormentors scattered.

Will rushed to Luigi's aid. The pastafarian pushed him away angrily. "Wassamatter? You want to cause more trouble? You want to trip Luigi up again, heh?"

"No!" Will helped the dazed pastafarian to his feet. Luigi stood swaying and rubbing his head. "Those halfwits aren't my friends. I'm sorry they treated you like that."

"Heh, you's a good boy." Luigi shook his head, trying to focus. "I'm hokay, I'm hokay, just let me get on with my job." He bent down to pick up a pizza box – and fell over again.

Will helped him stagger to the cart. "Look, you just sit here and wait. I'll deliver your pizzas for you."

Luigi gave him a dazed smile. "Verra good. You help Luigi. The names is written on the boxes, hokay?"

"OK." Will snatched up an armful of boxes and sped off.

The delivery took some time. Luigi's handwriting was a bit erratic and Will had to squint furiously.

On the last box, the writing was particularly hard to make out. Will held it up to Luigi. "Who's this one for?"

The pastafarian was still looking dazed. "One special Pizza Ferrari," he said faintly. "Humfrey the Boggart, Spindleshanks Tower."

"Pizza Ferrari?"

"Sure. Is-a fast food."

Will nodded and raced off. Luigi suddenly jerked upright as a thought struck him. "Hey, ma friend!" he called. "I'll do that one, no need for you to..."

But Will was already out of earshot. Luigi slumped on his seat and held his head in his hands. "O boys, o boys," he muttered. "The boss, he's no' going to like this."

Spindleshanks Tower was in the oldest and least frequented part of the castle. It was so called because of the two huge, gnarled wooden props holding it up, that made it look like an old man standing on crooked legs. Will pushed open a creaking door and trudged up a spiral staircase. Up and up he went as the stairs twisted and turned. Eventually he reached the top and stood before a heavy-looking wooden door. Balancing the pizza box on one hand, Will knocked on the door and waited.

After a few seconds he knocked again.

"All right, all right..." mumbled a voice from behind the door. Will heard a key being turned in a lock.

Then another. And another.

He waited as a series of small, muffled, metallic clunks rang out as bolts shot back. This customer was certainly security conscious, thought Will. Finally, there was the clinking sound of several chains being drawn across the door.

Will continued to wait.

Eventually, the door opened a crack. A suspicious-looking eye peered out, at about the level of Will's knee.

"Whaddaya want, kid?" The voice had a rasping quality, with a suggestion of a lisp.

"Pizza," Will told the eye.

"I ain't got any."

"No, I'm delivering a pizza. From Luigi."

"Oh, yeah." The eye darted a glance behind Will. "You been followed?"

Followed? wondered Will. Why should he have been followed? He shook his head.

"OK, come in." The door opened.

Will stepped into the dark room. The door slammed behind him. He jumped and spun round. To his horror, Will found himself staring at the business end of a lethal-looking crossbow.

CHAPTER NINE

H ow Will met a boggart in Myshterioush Circumshtanshesh and how Will and Luigi were Accosted in The Crumbles.

"**P**ut the box down on the table, keep your hands where I can shee them and don't make any shudden movesh."

"Shudden movesh?" repeated Will.

"Shtand shtill."

Realisation hit Will. "Oh, you mean, don't make any sudden moves. You want me to stand still."

"That'sh what I said. What are you, shome kind of idiot?"

Will stared at the small figure. "Er... is this right?" he stammered, "Pizza for Mister Boggart?"

"I'll ashk the queshtionsh, kid. Where's Luigi?"

"He's outside. He got a bang on the head. I'm helping him out."

"That'sh too bad." To Will's relief the crossbow was lowered. "You're not shupposed to know I'm here."

"Are you Mr Boggart?"

"Thatsh me, shweetheart. Humfrey the Boggart, the besht Private Inqueshtigator in Dun Indewood." He took out a card from an inner pocket and handed it to Will.

Humfrey the Boggart
Pryvate Inquestigator
People watched. Things found. Secrecy assured.
The Best for a Quest, Forget the Rest

Will was impressed. "Are there many private inquestigators in Dun Indewood?" he asked, putting the pizza box on the table.

Humfrey gave a self-congratulatory smile. "I'm the only one."

Will nodded. "No offence, but aren't boggarts supposed to live in the Forest? I thought you weren't allowed in the City."

Humfrey grimaced. "Thanksh for remindin' me, kid. Yeah, all goblinsh, gnomesh, trollsh, dwarvesh, elvesh, pixiesh, boggartsh, etshetera, etshetera are banned from Dun Indewood on the orders of Gordin, the big cheese himshelf, on pain of death, torture and pain, not neccesharily in that order. Tell me shomething I don't know." Humfrey jerked his thumb at the dingy room. "Why d'you think I'm holed up in thish crummy joint? I'm workin' undercover."

Will's eyes lit up. Although the boggart was about half Will's height, he looked a hard-boiled character. His face was unshaven, jowly and lopsided and he had rather sad eyes; but his job sounded exciting. "Are you inquestigating someone now?" Will asked excitedly.

"Letsh put it thish way," replied Humfrey. "I keep my eyesh and earsh open. I got my shushpishionsh."

"Shushpishionsh?" Will frowned. "Oh, you mean suspicions."

The boggart glared at him. "That's what I shaid, shushpishionsh." His eyes narrowed. "Hey, kid, you got a rip in your tunic there. Let me fix that for ya." He turned back the collar of his cloak and pulled out a needle, already threaded.

Will sat in stunned silence while the boggart gathered the torn edges with lightning quick, expert stitches. "Er – is this the right time for needlework?"

Humfrey gave him an apologetic look. "I'm a boggart, shee," he said in a sulky voice. "Keeping things neat and tidy is what boggarts do. I guess you'd call it a kind of compulshion." The boggart bit the end off the thread, stuck the needle back in his collar and moved to the table. He opened the pizza box. "Looksh shcrummy." He pulled out a purse and emptied it into Will's outstretched hand.

Will counted the coins. "I think you're a little short." He looked down at the boggart's furious scowl and hastily added, "I mean you haven't given me enough money, not that you're..." he tailed off.

"Don't get shmart with me, beanpole, not unlesh you wanna go home with your shinsh in a shling. Tell Luigi I'll have to owe him." The boggart ushered Will to the door. "If you ever need my servicesh, my rates are fifty florinsh a day, plush exshpenshesh."

Will mentally translated. "Expenses?"

"Right. And remember, you ain't sheen me, OK? Now shcram. I gotta pizza gettin' cold here."

The door shut firmly behind Will who shook his head and made his way back down the stairs.

Luigi gave Will a sidelong look as he returned across the courtyard. "Hokay?"

Will nodded in a preoccupied way. "Um, OK, yes..."

Luigi began to say something, then thought better of it. "Hokay. I go now."

Will gave him an anxious look. "Are you sure you can drive? You still look a bit woozy."

"Sure I can drive." Luigi gave the reins an expert flick and the dogcart went backwards into the wall.

"Move over," said Will. "I'll drive."

A pair of guards opened the huge, iron-bound wooden gates intended to keep the castle safe from the inhabitants of the City (though in Symon's case, thought Will sourly, they served to protect the City from the inhabitants of the castle). The dogcart trundled out into the gathering darkness.

Will clicked his tongue and flicked the reins. "Good

dog." The dog turned its head and gave him a tongue-lolling grin.

"Tha's Hot Dog," Luigi told Will.

"Hot dog?"

"Sure. While I'm deliverin' pizzas, he stands in the street pantin' an' people says, 'My word, your dog looks hot,' an' I say, 'Sure, he's a hot dog!' I guess the name kinda got stuck."

The cart trundled down the hill into the City of Dun Indewood.

Unnoticed by Luigi or Will, a tall man in a brown, threadbare cloak stepped out of an alley opposite the castle gates. His face was invisible under a deep hood; but the unseen eyes seemed to be watching the cart.

Luigi checked his delivery list. "Only one more call to make, now. We gotta head over the river to the left bank." Will obediently turned the dogcart down a side road towards Tanners' Trickle.

Dun Indewood was a City of two halves. It was divided by the Trickle that coursed its way through the very centre of the City. On the Eastern bank of the Trickle stood the ancient township of Right Indewood, with the castle and its surrounding districts, the homes of the fashionable, the successful and the well off.

In contrast, the Western bank of the City was made up

of dark, narrow alley-ways, squalid hovels and motley dwellings. It had once been known as the Rotten Bailiwick of Left Indewood.

For centuries, the inhabitants of Right and Left Indewood had stared at each other across the Trickle. The wealthy Right Bankers looked down on the poorer Left Bankers and the Left Bankers thought the Right Bankers were a bunch of stuck-up toffs.

Night had fallen, but the streets on the right bank still thronged with prosperous merchants, fat traders and idle young men in expensive clothes, with more money than chin. Will and Luigi soon reached the crumbling stone bridge over Tanners' Trickle.

As they crossed, Will looked down at the thin, greasy stream and wrinkled his nose. "Why bother to build a bridge over that?" he asked morosely.

Luigi shook a finger at Will. "You ever tried to wade through the Trickle? No? Well, don't, not if you wan' your feet to come out the same colour they went in."

"All right," said Will, "but why does the bridge have to be so big?"

"Ah, that's 'cos the Trickle din' used to be like this, accordin' to the stories. Years ago, it was one 'eck of a big river; all kin's a boats an' barges used to come up here, sailing-like, bringing goods an' travellers from foreign lands."

As the cart trundled over the bridge, Luigi warmed to his theme. The Trickle, he told Will, had once been a mighty waterway. Many of the legends of the City had begun in its swirling eddies, as questing Knyghts and intrepid sailors set off on their adventures from its busy quays and wharves. Months and years later, a handful of these brave souls might return with outlandish and mind-boggling stories of strange parts and wild creatures, and wild creatures with strange parts. But, like the glory days of Dun Indewood, the river had dried up. Nowadays only children's boats floated on the Trickle, slowly dissolving in its foul, acidic waters.

"Do you think the stories are true?" asked Will.

"Sure!" cried Luigi. "My Momma an' Poppa tol' me that my great, great, great, great ancestors arrived on a boat. They set up the first pasta restaurant in Dun Indewood. Sellin' to sailors and all kin's a river people."

"Is that right?" Will gave Luigi an apologetic grin. "I'm sorry, I don't know much about pastafarians."

"Well, we's called pastafarians on account of how we knows the secret of 'faring' – tha's an old-fashioned word for 'making' – pasta. Pasta-farian, see?" Luigi drew himself up proudly.

"But aren't you the only pastafarian around?" Will asked.

Luigi gave him a broad grin. "No – I'm just the only one left in Dun Indewood." Will looked blank. "My Momma an' Poppa tol' me there's pastafarians in every city, all in the food business."

"What other cities? Other cities are just legends. Nobody knows if they exist."

Luigi shrugged. "I couldn' say. But what I know is, if

there are other cities, you'll find a pasta restaurant in every one. We pastafarians, there's no' many of us anywhere, but there's some of us *everywhere*."

The final delivery was deep inside the forbidding district of The Grumbles. Will was glad that Luigi was with him. Normally, he wouldn't go near the area. It was home to hundreds of people you wouldn't want to meet in a dark alley. Unfortunately, The Grumbles was *all* dark alleys.

The street names added to The Grumbles' sense of inevitability: the Street of a Hundred Purse-snatchers, the Avenue of a Thousand Pickpockets, Muggers' Alley and Dead End. You couldn't say you weren't warned when you entered The Grumbles.

"I don' like this place." Luigi eyed the hard-faced inhabitants of The Grumbles who were lurking furtively in alley-ways, on the lookout for victims. "I don' like leavin' the cart round here. I always afraid that, when I get back, I find Hot Dog sittin' on lil' piles a bricks an' somebody taken all his legs off."

There was little light. Even moonlight didn't dare to creep into The Grumbles in case it couldn't get out again. Tall, ramshackle dwellings with overhanging roofs and impossibly narrow alley-ways added to the general air of claustrophobia.

As he drove through the maze-like streets, Will was vaguely aware of dark, shadowy figures in side alleys and doorways. He felt as though a hundred eyes were staring at him. Fear gripped at his stomach and his breathing became faster.

They rounded a corner – and Hot Dog skidded to a halt.

The road was blocked by three men.

At least, Will thought, I suppose they must be men. Trolls aren't as ugly, and ogres don't look as stupid.

"Well, well, well, what 'ave we got 'ere?" a rough voice growled.

"They should watch where they're goin'," rumbled a second voice, 'uvverwise they won't get there."

"I don't fink they'll get there anyway," a third rasped, "on account of I'm goin' to cut their legs off."

Three voices went "Hur hur hur."

Hot Dog gave a whine and tried to crawl backwards underneath the cart. Luigi waved his arms about. "Come on now, boys, be nice-like. I just gotta pizza delivery to make here..."

One of the thugs threw a heavy club. It whizzed through the air and caught Luigi on the side of the head. A look of deep disgust crossed Luigi's face. "Not again!" The pastafarian's eyes crossed and he slumped in his seat.

CHAPTER TEN

Of the many and diverse forms of Pasta and how Will was Sore Beset by a Vengeful Mob.

Will tried to stand. An arm like a tree trunk dragged him from the cart and a steel-tipped boot pushed him down on to the cobbles.

"I wonder if 'e's got any money."

"I dunno. Let's kick 'im and see if anyfing goes 'ching'."

"I haven't got any money!" snarled Will.

"Well, that settles it. I fink I'll just cut 'is froat." The first thief held out a cruel-looking knife. Will's eyes stared helplessly back at him from the polished steel of its blade. He seemed to be making a habit of being threatened with dangerous weapons.

"OK, bushter, put the knife down and move back shlowly." Humfrey the Boggart stepped out of a dark alley-way. His crossbow nestled easily in his hands.

"Now, I know what you're thinkin'," he drawled. "Thish is a shingle-shot bow, so I can only take out one of you. But the queshtion is, which one?" He stared steadily at the silent thieves. "So what you gotta ashk yourshelvesh is, do I feel lucky?" His eyes narrowed menacingly. "Well, do ya, punksh?"

Will gaped at Humfrey. He heard the clatter of a knife blade striking the cobbles behind him. He spun round. The street was empty. The thieves had gone.

Humfrey reached into his purse and pulled out a coin, which he flipped towards Will, who caught it automatically.

"Thought I had shome more change shomewhere." The boggart pulled down the brim of his hat. "Be sheein' you, kid."

He stepped back into the alley and was gone.

Shaking his head with bewilderment, Will staggered to his feet and went back to the cart to revive Luigi.

Some time later, Will turned the cart into the main square in the fashionable district of Beau Monde. He pulled up in front of a cheerful-looking, white-painted building with little tables outside. A large sign above the door read: *Luigi's Fasta Pasta on the Piazza.*

Luigi hadn't stopped talking since Will had revived him (for the second time that day). "I still can't believe it! There was three of them, three big, ver' bad men, an' you sent them runnin' home to their mammas!" To Will's intense embarrassment, Luigi gave him a big hug and kissed him on both cheeks.

"I keep telling you, Luigi," he protested weakly, "I didn't do anything, it was Humfrey…"

"Sure, sure, it was a little bitty boggart…" Luigi beamed at Will and waved towards the tables. "Sit, sit. I put the cart away, I open up the restaurant, then we eat." As he bustled off, Will gave an exasperated sigh, then wandered over to the menu board. After all, it was late, and he'd missed supper at the Knyght School. Squinting hard, and forming the words with his lips, he read:

*Pasta and piece a'Pizza on the Piazza,
You can'ta get fasta!*
Spaghetti
Cannawormi
Wobblijelli
Pavarotti
Faitaccompli
Gucci
Armani
All with Bordercolli or Presto Sauce

Luigi erupted from the depths of his restaurant carrying two large plates piled high with pasta and meatballs. "Here you go! Luigi's Pasta Blasta!"

Will was still struggling to read the menu board. "What's Cannawormi?"

"Pasta inna shape of lil' worms."

"And Pavarotti?"

"Pasta inna shape of a big open mouth…"

Will ran his eyes down the menu again. "Is this all pasta?"

"Sure. Pasta's pasta! It all look diff'rent, but it all taste the same." Luigi grinned happily and took an enormous mouthful of variously shaped pasta and tomato sauce. "Sit, sit!" He solemnly wiped his right hand on his apron and held it out to Will. "You save my life tonight, prob'ly. You an' me, we's friends."

Will grinned weakly and shook Luigi's hand. It seemed the easiest thing to do.

From a shadowy doorway across the square, two figures watched Will and Luigi tuck into their meal.

"I looked after the kid, bossh, just like you shaid," drawled the shorter of the two.

The taller figure nodded slowly and pulled its hood down further.

"You want I should shtill keep an eye out for him?"

The taller figure nodded.

"You want I should keep watchin' You Know Who?"

The figure nodded again.

Humfrey felt in his pocket. "You want a shlice of cold pizza?"

"Or would you rather eat donkey brains fried in lard?" said a sarcastic voice from the bag slung across the tall figure's back. The hood turned towards the boggart. Cold eyes glinted in its depths.

"Forget I ashked."

The following day, Will was beaten for leaving the Knyght School without permission. However, it seemed pretty tame after years of thrashings from Doctor Blud. It was much less easy to deal with the antagonism of his fellow students.

Most of his chief tormentors were too cowardly to take Will on face to face, and those who tried quickly learned that driving bears and wolves away from his pigs had made him pretty handy in a fight. Still, they did what they could to make Will's days unpleasant with surreptitious kicks, punches and name-calling.

Will tried not to let this bother him. He was used to being called rude names, and not having many friends; but he was still grateful for Gyles' companionship. However, one day, as he was walking down the corridor outside Gyles' study, he heard voices coming through the open door.

"You're starting to stink, Gyles." Will recognised the sneering voice as Symon's. "That's what comes of hanging about with pig boys."

"Leave me alone." Gyles' voice was unsteady.

"We don't like people who make friends with pig boys, do we, Jervaise?"

"No." Jervaise's deep voice rumbled with menace.

Will was just about to burst through the door and leap

to Gyles' defence when he heard him squeak, "Who says he's my friend?"

Will froze. He heard Symon's voice saying in mock surprise, "Isn't he?"

"Not really." Gyles was trying to sound offhand. "I just felt sorry for him, if you must know."

Will didn't wait to hear any more. He walked quietly away feeling sick and angry. He knew Gyles was frightened and hadn't meant what he'd said. But he'd said it. A true Knyght would never betray a friend. Will felt sorry for Gyles, but he couldn't forgive him.

Although Will didn't escape the malice of the other pupils in lessons, it was in the dormitories that they had most scope to play ill-natured pranks on him. Will often found his bed soaked with water (or worse), but since he seemed perfectly happy to make a bedroll out of his clothes and sleep on the floor (it was less draughty than his bed at home, and not much harder), his enemies soon grew tired of these tricks. During the evenings, Will often took refuge in exploring the forgotten rooms of the castle, or reading about the history of Dun Indewood and the deeds of its Knyghts in the library.

Jervaise deLacey hated Will for beating him at jousting and Symon had never forgiven Will for, according to Symon's version of events, getting him in trouble with his father over the Tournament. But knowing they were no match for Will, they contented themselves with trying to make his life miserable in small ways, and waited, biding their time until they and a sufficient number of cronies could get Will on his own.

Their opportunity came on Founder's Day. This was the celebration of the establishment of the Knyght School by its first Headmaster, Sir Montgummery Founder, and was viewed by the staff as an opportunity to celebrate the achievements of the school, past and present, and, more importantly, to eat a big meal and drink too much.

By late evening, all the staff were snoozing in armchairs (or wherever else they happened to pass out). Will was sitting in the darkened library, reading the *I Espy Book of Dragons*, when Gyles came racing in and grabbed him by the arm.

Will gave him a cold look. "What do you want?"

Gyles was out of breath and looked guilty and unhappy. "Look, I know I've not been a good friend, but I *have* come to warn you…"

"What about?"

"Symon and Jervaise deLacey have got a bunch of their pals together." Gyles cast a nervous glance over his shoulder. "They're coming to get you. You'd better hide," he went on, as the noise of the approaching mob began to echo down the corridor. "They're going to toss you in a blanket…"

Will shrugged. "That doesn't sound too bad."

"…They're going to toss you, in a blanket, off the battlements."

The mob outside was closer now, and baying for blood. Will hesitated for a moment, then ran for the door.

"There he is!"

There followed a breakneck chase through the rooms and corridors of the Knyght School. Will sped across the tilting yard and then up through the deserted classrooms and dormitories with the mob at his heels. Most of his pursuers were out of condition, and it wasn't hard for Will to outdistance them, but he needed to draw them away from the school gates; then he could double back and escape.

However, when Will wrenched open a door on to the walkway on top of the castle walls, he discovered that he had underestimated his enemy's cunning. Symon had split his forces. Will raced along the battlements in the moonlight – and came to a dead halt as a door in front of him was thrust open. A pack of boys led by Jervaise emerged, howling with triumph. Will turned back, only to find that his pursuers had caught up with him. Symon, well to the rear, brandished a blanket and gave an evil chuckle.

"Look to yourself, pig boy," he snarled.

Will kept his voice level. "If you have a quarrel with me, Symon, come and fight."

Symon spat. "I don't fight pig boys."

"Or anyone else," said Will. He glanced over the wall; a long drop lay behind him. A broken leg for sure – maybe a broken neck.

Symon gave a snarl of hate. "Get him!"

Will braced himself, determined to take some of them with him – but as the attackers hesitated, there was a sudden burst of dazzling light. Boys shielded their eyes and cried out as a figure in a long, travel-stained robe pushed through the mob and came to Will's side.

The newcomer had an oddly-shaped pack on his back. He was holding aloft something that shone with a cool, unearthly brilliance. He threw back his hood. Though half-blinded by the glare, Will at once recognised the old man who had spoken up for him at the Tournament.

"Wretches, for shame!" he cried in a ringing voice. "Thirty of thee against a single lad and he unarmed."

Symon, who could be quite brave when he was speaking to old men – as long as he was surrounded by his minions – yelled, "That is no business of yours, greybeard! Who do you think you are?"

The old man eyed him as he might have looked at a slug. "Why, as to that," he said softly, "I am called the Runemaster."

His backpack gave a gleeful cackle. "Roll of drums!" it cried. "Ta-daaaa!"

Thirty pairs of eyes bulged in shock. Thirty mouths dropped open. Thirty seconds later, the battlements were deserted except for the Runemaster and Will, who stood staring at the strange, smiling figure as the light in his hand died and the stars slowly reappeared in the night sky.

CHAPTER ELEVEN

How the Runemaster (despite his companion's Harping On) addressed the Great Council of Dun Indewood and gave them What For.

The Great Hall of the Castle of Dun Indewood was packed to the rafters. Statues of dead kings peered stonily down from their niches around the walls. The High Lord, Gordin, sat on his Chair of State, to the right of the empty Throne of the Kings. On rows of benches below him sat his Earls, Lords and Counsellors in their rich crimson robes edged with fur. (Much of this had a suspiciously tabby look about it. Since nobody went hunting in the Forest these days, the fur of wild animals was hard to come by, and Dun Indewood's cats had taken to going around in pairs and looking behind them nervously.)

In serried ranks below them sat the Knyghts, each wearing a surcoat emblazoned with his coat of arms. The Ladies of the Court sat to either side, beneath faded banners that fluttered sadly in the many draughts from broken windows set in cracked frames. The boys and staff of the Knyght School huddled at the other end of the Hall, in pews made of dark-stained wood that formed a sort of pen. There was absolute silence. You could have a heard a pin drop.

Ping!

"Pick that pin up, you nasty noisy numbskull of a bally boy," hissed Sir Regynild, "and don't let me catch you playing with it again!"

Gyles blushed. "Sorry, sir," he muttered.

Into the silence swept the Runemaster. He was still wearing his travel-stained, homespun brown cloak. His hood was thrown back, revealing his shock of snow-white hair. In all that colourful, gorgeously dressed assembly, he should have appeared poor and shabby; but though he looked like a peasant, he walked like a king. He wasn't the sort of old man Symon and his cronies liked to tease in the market square. He was the sort of old man who, when he looked at you, made you wish your shoes were cleaner and you'd taken the trouble to wash behind your ears. His gaze, sweeping round the room, left a chill wherever it fell.

The Runemaster shrugged off the strange, triangular-shaped bag he carried across his shoulders and put it down carefully. Then he bowed to Gordin. "My Lord, thou knowest who I am."

Gordin's answering bow was little more than a nod

of the head, and his voice was harsh. "I know who you claim to be."

"Oh, he's him, all right," said a voice from the bag. "Take it from me. I'd know the old curmudgeon anywhere."

The Runemaster frowned and hissed at the bag, "When I need thee to vouch for me, I will ask thee."

"Well, pardon me for vibrating," it retorted. "Do you want me here as a witness, or not?"

With a sigh, the Runemaster opened the bag and drew out a beautifully-crafted harp. It had a head carved at the top, wearing a crown; but the face was set in a disagreeable sneer. "Behold the Harp of the Kings," said the Runemaster without enthusiasm.

The carved head, although it had no neck, somehow swivelled to face the assembly. "That's me," it rasped. "Don't bother with the prolonged applause." The head turned back to the Runemaster. "Are we going to get on with this or what?"

The Runemaster hadn't ordered, or even requested, a gathering (the first for many years) of the Great Council of Dun Indewood. He had simply made it known that he wished to speak to the Council of the City. The council had assembled to hear him, mostly from curiosity and in the hope of being entertained. The folk of Dun Indewood, after all, didn't get out much. In fact, thought Will, sitting next to Gyles on the very back row of the Knyght School benches, they didn't get out at all. He leaned forward in fascination to listen to what the Runemaster – and his strange companion – had to say.

The old man raised his voice. "Lords, Knyghts and Squires of Dun Indewood. Thou hast heard of the Runemaster. Thou knowest that he was once the Chief Wizard of the City."

"Oh, yes," drawled the Harp, "big deal. You were about as popular as a hedgehog in a balloon factory and for pretty much the same reason – you kept making things go BANG and vanish. Admit it."

The Runemaster pointedly ignored the instrument. "Thou hast heard," he went on, "that the Runemaster disappeared many years ago. Thou mayest have heard…" Here, his glance rested for a moment on Gordin, "…that he left on a hopeless Quest; a fool's errand. Thou mayest have heard that he perished miserably in the Dark Forest. Thou mayest even have heard that he never really existed. But he did exist. He survived the Quest. And now, he stands before thee!"

"Two cheers," said the Harp snidely. "Limited rejoicings."

There were confused murmurs. Few members of the assembly recognised the Runemaster. Many of the stupider ones started looking round as if they expected someone in a pointed hat to appear suddenly in a puff of smoke.

Professor Bone, who had nodded off, woke up with a start and bellowed, "Who? Where? What?" while younger members of staff tried to shush him.

The old man shook his head impatiently. "No, no, no!" he snapped. "I mean, I am he. I am the Runemaster."

There were shamefaced mutters along the lines of, "Oh, right!" and "I knew that." Professor Bone grumbled,

"Damfool should've said so in the first place," and went to sleep again.

"He disappeared donkey's years ago," Gyles whispered out of the corner of his mouth. "I thought he was only a legend. Wonder where he's been?"

The Runemaster's eyes glittered angrily. "I left this hall many years ago on a Quest to restore the greatest treasure of the City. I swore I would not return until I had the salvation of Dun Indewood in my hands. Now I have returned, and what do I find?" He waved a hand towards the high windows, through which the gaunt remains of the citadel loomed like a huge broken tooth. "The Citadel of the Kings a crumbling ruin, its proud halls abandoned to the ravages of time and the elements."

Muttering broke out again. The nobility of Dun Indewood didn't take kindly to being criticised.

The Runemaster ignored the interruption. His gaze swept the Hall. "I find the Castle of the High Lords a dust-filled relic, unused, uncared for; its banners mouldering, its treasures lost, its glories fading into decay."

The Harp gave a theatrical sigh. "You're breaking my heart," it said sarcastically. Will noticed that its strings vibrated as it spoke, producing the sound.

The Runemaster ignored it. His contemptuous gaze fell on the assembled nobility of the City. "Worst of all, I find the sad and spineless remains of a once-proud people. The Lords and Knyghts of Dun Indewood, a parcel of slug-a-beds with bodies grown fat with gluttony and sloth, whose weapons rust in their sheaths."

The Harp cackled. "That's tellin' 'em, Runie!"

Gyles gave an appalled giggle. "Oh, what a dreadful thing to say!"

Will snorted. "Well, it's true, isn't it?"

"No, of course not – this is just a... um..." Gyles' voice took on a sing-song quality as if he was repeating a lesson learned by rote. "...a period of respite, during which we are gathering our strength for the great task ahead."

Will strongly suspected that the Knyghts of Dun Indewood would go right on gathering their strength even if the City was attacked by an army of dragons (though probably from under their beds rather than in them). His heart was pounding. At last, here was someone with the courage to say what needed to be said. He glanced around. Some of the boys were staring at the speaker with blank incomprehension. Others, like Gyles, were in a state of delighted horror at the spectacle of their elders and betters getting a good ticking off; but many more looked indignant and hostile.

The Runemaster was forced to raise his voice against the growing protest. "And the poison spreads outwards from the heart. For many weeks since my return, I have walked unknown through the City. I have questioned, I have observed, I have even interfered."

"Oh, brother!" sneered the Harp. "Has he ever interfered!"

Gyles tugged Will's sleeve. "He means the Tournament! When he stopped Gordin from hanging you! I was there!" Will glared Gyles into silence as the Runemaster continued:

"Everything I have learnt has filled me with dismay, because everywhere in the City, I have found greed, faithlessness and cruelty."

There were howls of derision. Knyghts stamped their feet and hooted, wizened old counsellors waved their fists, boys whistled and catcalled, ladies (feeling it was expected of them) had fainting fits.

The Harp's face curved into a malicious grin. "You're not making any friends here. You know that, don't you?" it chortled. The Runemaster quelled it with a look and glared round at the throng until the protests had died down to sullen muttering.

"I shall say no more of thy decline and degradation," he said quietly. "Now, I shall speak of thy salvation."

The mutters died into silence. The council craned to listen. They'd had enough insults, but if this rude old man had something to offer them, they were prepared to overlook his bad manners – provided that getting it didn't involve any effort or cost them money.

The Runemaster raised his head. His voice carried to every corner of the Great Hall. "I left the City in search of the greatest treasure of Dun Indewood…"

"Hey, hey, hey!" The Harp's voice cut in sharply. "You're talking about the Quest, right? That's my job. All tales of Quests, Sagas or Adventures told through Praise Songs, Ballads and Lays are the rightful narrative property of Bards, Minstrels, Troubadors and their instruments, including harps, to wit, me. I get to tell them about the Quest. Check my contract."

The Runemaster gave a hollow groan. "If thou must."

"Right, where did you get to? Left the City... got it, got it. Right." The Harp's strings played a jangling march and it sang:

"*Long was the way and hard the Quest...*"

"Hard!" The Harp played a crashing discord and its voice reverted to its usual complaining whine. "Hard! Don't get me started... where was I?"

The Runemaster opened his mouth to speak. "I know, I know," snapped the Harp, "don't tell me!" The tune began again.

"*He trod the road with little rest.*
Through dangers dark, o'er country bare,
In faltering hope and black despair
    (*good grief, who writes this stuff?*)
He journeyed on..."

(with me bouncing along on his bony back every step of the way, I might add, and did I get tuned occasionally? Did I get a wipe over with linseed oil? I don't *think* so. Anyway...)

Beset by ogres, through thick snow
And killing frost his trail did go,
To something-something-something shores
Past hairy things with big sharp claws...
    Erm...
Te dum te dum te dum te dee..."

The Harp tailed off. The tune jangled to silence. Its lips moved for a moment, and then it gave a bright smile and said, "Well, you get the general idea. To cut a long story short, he found what he was looking for and came back here, the end." The Harp stood silent, with a smug look on its face.

The Runemaster passed a hand over his eyes. "Hast thou quite finished?"

The Harp was offended. "What's your problem, Mister Picky? Some people just don't know a classy narrative when they hear one." Its strings thrummed a disagreeable note while the Knyghts fidgeted. They didn't like all this stuff about long, hard Quests – some fool might take it into his head that facing dangers and hardships was what Knyghts were supposed to do, and then where would they be?

The Runemaster rallied. "No more of that. I prevailed. I found the lost treasure of the City and I have brought it back unto thee." He reached inside his cloak and took hold of a chain. Lifting it from round his neck, he held the prize above his head.

"Behold, the Dragonsbane!"

Chapter Twelve

How the Great Council was most
Underwhelmed and of the Runes with
a View.

If the Runemaster had expected cries of joy and wonder, he was disappointed. A heavy-looking stone hung from a clasp on the end of the chain. It was the size of a man's fist and had a dull, milky-white surface. Even Will had to admit it didn't really look anything special.

One of the court ladies tittered and said very audibly to her friend, "Well, I suppose it might look all right on him. I wouldn't be seen dead wearing it." The assembly broke into a chorus of ill-natured guffaws.

The Harp looked up at the Runemaster. "That didn't go over big," it said nastily. "I'd cut to the song, if I were you."

Lord Gordin leaned forward. His eyes were mere slits. His voice was charged with malice. "So this is the great treasure that has kept you from your duties for so long," he said. "And pray tell us: what is the significance of this... bauble?"

The Runemaster stared at Gordin until the sneer left the High Lord's face and he shifted uneasily in his seat.

"This stone..." The words seemed to be dragged out from the old man like coins from a miser's purse. "...This stone has been, from time beyond reckoning, the source of all the might and majesty of the Kings of Dun Indewood. For the power of the stone is this." His voice grew stronger, and rang through the Hall. "He who wields the stone has the power to summon dragons and bind them to his will."

"If that's your idea of a good time," added the Harp.

There was dead silence for a moment, followed by a lot of coughing and shuffling. Lords and Knyghts looked at their feet, out of the window – anywhere but at the Runemaster or each other. Several ladies had quiet hysterics.

The Runemaster gazed about him, his look of triumph fading into one of bewilderment and disbelief. "What is amiss?" he said slowly. "Can it be that the council scorns my gift?" He turned to Gordin, who was silently watching him through hooded eyes.

Several members of the council were pushing and prodding each other, like boys summoned to the Head's study to explain exactly how they'd managed to kick a football through his window. There were hisses of, "You tell him...", "No, you...". Eventually, Old Lord Robat fitzBadly was thrust forward. He stood blinking at the Runemaster and clearing his throat nervously.

"Um... this Dragonsbane thingy," he began in a worried voice. "I mean, frightfully decent of you to bring it back and all that sort of thing, much appreciated I'm sure, but... er... isn't it a bit... well... dangerous?"

"Dangerous?" The Runemaster's voice was hardly a whisper.

"Well, I mean, dragons, don'cher know... vicious things from what one hears, covered with scales and breathing fire and whatnot. I mean, does anybody really want to summon one, when it comes right down to it? And as for binding it to yer will, oh, yes, well, it's easy to talk. I had a wolfhound once, trained it meself, could've sworn I had it bound to me will like anything. Then, before you could say 'Bad Dog', the wretched beast was widdling on the furniture and when I took a rolled-up scroll to it, the dam' thing nearly had me leg orf."

The Runemaster looked around bleakly. "And is this the will of you all?"

There was more shuffling. Nobody spoke.

The Harp grinned spitefully. "I think you can take that as a 'yes'."

The Runemaster remained still for a moment, slumped in defeat. He looked old and tired. Will bit his lip. Lord Gordin's expression was carefully blank, but a muscle in his cheek twitched.

Then the Runemaster straightened. Once more, his proud glance swept round the room. "So be it," he said calmly.

Then he turned, picked up the Harp and strode from the Great Hall.

"Hey! Where are we going? What about my closing number? I haven't told them about all the spells you messed up, or how you got thrown out of that tavern, or..." The Harp's complaining voice faded.

Everyone started talking at once, their voices echoing through the hall: "Good riddance, if you ask me..." "Silly old fool..." "Dragons! What was the feller thinkin' of?" "'Course, I'd've summoned a dragon like a shot if I'd been thirty years younger..." "Dashed bad form, frightnin' the ladies..."

Will barely heard them. He pushed through the ranks of his schoolmates and vaulted over the front of their enclosure. Pursued by cries of, "You, boy! Bring your beastly bally body back here at once, you boil-faced barbarian!" from Sir Regynild, he raced through the crowd in the wake of the Runemaster.

The afternoon had faded to dusk and the empty courtyard of the castle was filled with shadows. Will halted, panting, and stared about him. Where could the Runemaster have gone?

There was a dull clatter from the darkness ahead of him; a foot had caught a loose stone and sent it skittering over the rough cobbles of the yard. Will hurried forwards. As his eyes adjusted to the dim light, he realised where he was. High above him loomed the broken mass of the citadel. Before him stood the gateway to the ancient fortress, the door he had so often longed to pass through.

It hung slightly open, creaking softly in the breeze.

Heart thumping, Will crept inside.

The citadel was dark, and utterly silent. The floor was uneven and covered with stones which had fallen from the high walls in ages past. Rank grasses pushed through gaps between the stones and lichen grew on the naked granite walls. Somewhere, water dripped slowly into an echoing pool.

Hardly breathing, Will felt his way forward. A black shape rocketed out from a ledge and flew at his face with a shriek. Will cried out and staggered back, but it was only a raven which turned aside and fled, croaking in derision. Doggedly, Will crept on until he reached a crumbling stairway. He turned to one side and came face to face with a dragon.

It was several heart-stopping seconds before Will realised that the creature was made of stone. Even so, it was terrifying. It stood poised to leap, its claws ready to strike, its great wings half-unfurled. Its reptilian lips were pulled back in a snarl, revealing teeth like daggers and its forked tongue licked out beyond its sharp, wicked-looking muzzle. Its dull stone eyes stared at him implacably, probing his deepest secrets and desires.

Will turned again. A mirror image of the first dragon guarded the other side of the stair; but the years had been less kind to this second statue. Its great stone head, with one of its wings, had been smashed from its body by falling stones and lay tumbled at its feet.

Will forced his unsteady legs to carry him up the wide stairs and through the archway at their head. He sensed a huge space around him as he peered into the gloom.

Then a brilliant light seemed to explode before him and the shadows leapt back. Half blinded, Will made out the figure of the Runemaster standing in the centre of a vast, ruinous hall, its roof open to the sky. The old man had his back to Will and he held aloft the Dragonsbane. The stone, swinging on its chain, shone with an unearthly radiance.

Without looking round, the Runemaster said, "Come in, Will. Welcome to the Citadel of the Kings."

The small fire sent shadows leaping and dancing across the dank stone walls of the citadel. Will had collected pieces of broken and decayed timber, the remains of the beams that had once carried the great vaulted roof of the stronghold of the Kings. Now he sat on one side of the fire. The Runemaster, with the Dragonsbane (dull and lifeless now) once more hanging from its chain around his neck, sat on the other. They were silent.

The Harp stood nearby, its carved mouth twisted into a sneer. "Well, isn't this jolly. Let's toast some crumpets and sing a merry campfire song."

Will looked up into the Runemaster's lined face. "I must thank you, sir," he said with awkward formality. "You saved my life. Twice."

"Three timesh." Humfrey the Boggart stepped out from a

wall niche, shaking cobwebs from his feather duster.

The Harp gave a delighted cackle at Will's shocked expression. "But who's counting?" it said archly.

Will stared from the boggart to the Runemaster. "Humfrey was working for you?"

"He catches on quickly for a simpleton," sniped the Harp.

Will ignored the jibe and shook his head. "I don't understand – why should you take all that trouble over me?"

"Because you're important, Will." Rose came in through the broken doors.

"Well, I'll be a banjo's uncle!" cheered the Harp ironically. "The gang's all here!" It played the sort of happy, bouncy tune that made everyone who heard it want to hit people, and sang:

> "Friends, friends, friends to the end
> Where would you be without friends?
> You are friends who'll never smother
> Stab or strangle one another
> You are all a band of brothers...

(apart from the one who's a sister; and let's face it, you bunch of sad losers had better be friends with each other...)

> 'Cos nobody else would be stupid enough
> To have any of you as friends...."

Rose stared at the Harp coldly. "You see that fire? You

see what's burning there? Wood. And what are you made of? Think about it before you make any more funny remarks."

"Well, excuuuuse me!" But the Harp's voice was less self-assured. It said no more, but kept casting nervous glances at Rose out of the corner of its carved wooden eyes.

The old man took a small bag from an inside pocket of his robe.

"Thou knowest I am called the Runemaster," he said to Will. "But perhaps thou dost not know what the title means?" Will shook his head.

"One of my powers..." the Runemaster gave the Harp, which was snickering under its breath, an angry glare. "One of my *many* powers is the ability to tell the future in the fall of the runes." He held out the bag to Will. "Here are the runes. Cast them. Thou shalt see what shall befall thee."

Feeling rather foolish, Will did so.

There was a short silence.

"I think," Rose said carefully, "that you're supposed to take the runes out of the bag before you throw them."

"Oh." Will blushed, retrieved the bag and opened it. He tipped a dozen small white stones into his hand. Each had a Rune carved into both sides. Will eyed the spiky letters curiously, then flicked his wrist to send them scattering across the floor.

There was a longer silence as the Runemaster studied the fall of the discs. Then he straightened up and exchanged significant looks with Humfrey and Rose.

"The message of the runes remains the same," he said quietly.

The Harp grunted. "Sez you." But the protest was subdued.

"The runes foretell that Dun Indewood is in grave danger." The Runemaster sighed. "What that danger is, and how it may be averted, they do not say. But on one point they are absolutely clear." He turned to look Will full in the face. "They tell of a young man of humble birth, who has endured suffering on another's behalf."

"In case you missed the point, chucklehead, he means you," the Harp told Will.

Will clicked his fingers. "That's why you dropped the poker when I told Rose I was Symon's whipping boy!"

"Indeed, at that moment I recognised thee. Thy destiny is laid out in the runes."

Will stared at Rose, at Humfrey and back at the Runemaster. "What must I do?" he asked quietly.

"Thou must undertake a desperate Quest. I cannot tell the object of the Quest, or where it will lead thee, or what its end will be. But thou must accomplish it or the whole of Dun Indewood will be destroyed."

"A Quest!" Will's eyes shone in the firelight.

The Runemaster stood, and to Will's astonishment, swept him a low bow. "The fate of the City is in your hands. Welcome to your destiny."

The Harp's voice echoed around the silent hall. "And you really are welcome to it. Believe me."

Chapter Thirteen

Of the True and Glorious History of the Most Precious Treasure of Dun Indewood, the Powerful and Majestic symbol of the City's Greatness, and how it was Nicked.

"But why me?" Will demanded for the hundredth time as he paced up and down the echoing stone floor of the Runemaster's study.

The morning after his arrival at the citadel, the Runemaster had discovered that all the rooms in the ruined fortress were lacking a roof, or had huge holes in the walls, or flooded when it rained – except for three small chambers which remained habitable.

The Runemaster had immediately taken possession of these. Gordin had made no objections; he had simply refused to aid the Runemaster in any way and had thereafter completely ignored him, continuing to govern the City from his palace in the castle as usual.

For his part, the Runemaster had asked nothing of the High Lord. Over the succeeding days, Will, Rose and Humfrey had scoured the City to find sticks of furniture and tapestries to make the bare chambers a bit more comfortable. Luigi and Hot Dog had obligingly delivered these to the citadel when they brought the guards' pizza orders to the castle. The pastafarian had even chipped in with one of his own restaurant tables, which, with its brightly upholstered chairs and umbrella advertising a popular drink, looked rather odd against the bare stone walls.

Will had been beaten again for leaving the hall at the end of the Great Council. After that, he had quietly gathered his few belongings, left his dormitory at the Knyght School and moved into the citadel. He hadn't discussed this with the Runemaster, who had made no comment when Will took over the smallest of the rooms. The old man used the second room as a bedchamber and the largest chamber as a study and meeting room.

This room was now as cheerful as a thorough cleaning (thanks to the boggart), moth-eaten wall-hangings and rickety furniture could make it. A roaring fire burned in the grate. A bubbling pan hung over it on a steel tripod. Dim light lanced down from slit windows high above and dust motes swirled in the shafts of sunlight.

The Runemaster sat at a wobbly table, poring over a selection of books Will had borrowed from the Knyght School library. Rose sat cross-legged on a rag carpet, gluing flight feathers on to the shafts of arrows, while the Harp stood in a corner, humming sarcastic little songs to itself.

Will paced up and down. "Why me?" he said again.

Rose gave him an exasperated look. "I can't imagine," she said crossly. A mischievous grin spread across her face. "After all, you're not of noble birth, you have few accomplishments..."

"Thank you," said Will, glaring at her.

"I mean," Rose went on, "you can't ride a horse or fight very well, can't do magic, you're not very bright..."

"Yes, thank you."

"You're not exactly Mr Muscles, you don't know your way around the Forest and you're not particularly brave..."

The Harp snickered.

"All right!" snapped Will. "I think you've made your point."

"Then stop asking, 'Why me?' Why not, for pity's sake?"

As Will relapsed into gloomy silence, the Runemaster looked up from his books. "To answer thy question, Will," he said slowly, "I believe that this Quest can only be completed by a person who is loyal and honourable and who really believes in what the Knyghts of Dun Indewood used to stand for. This will be a task, not for a deadly warrior or a cunning wizard – but for a Good Knyght."

Will tried not to look pleased. Rose rolled her eyes.

"Thish what you been lookin' for, boss?" Humfrey strolled in with his usual lack of ceremony and deposited a small scroll on the table. "I snitched it from Gordin'sh deshk." He busied himself tidying up the room.

The Runemaster read the cracked parchment. At

length, the old man gave a sigh and pushed the scroll away from him. Humfrey looked up from plumping some cushions and raised his eyebrows expectantly.

"It is as I suspected," said the Runemaster sighing again, "and as I feared."

Humfrey pursed his lips and gave the nod of a Private Inquestigator who is confirmed in his suspicions. "That'sh too bad." He took out a spotless handkerchief and started polishing a wine goblet.

Rose stepped behind the old man and put a hand protectively on his shoulder. The Runemaster reached up and patted Rose's hand. Then he became brisk. "Come! Draw your chairs up to the fire. It is time you all heard the full history of the Dragonsbane. Humfrey's discovery provides the last missing chapter of that story; now that I know the whole tale, it is time to pass it on."

When they were all settled before the fire (with Humfrey sorting the logs in the basket into order of size), the Runemaster began:

"From the foundation of the City, the Dragonsbane was the chief treasure of Dun Indewood. It is said that the stone was won by the first King, Bryun the Strong, who defeated the Dragon of the Fiery Wastes in single combat when it attacked the City. The victory cost him his life; and it was his son, Iyan the First, who cut out the dragon's heart. The heart turned to stone in his hands." The old man cupped the treasure in his hands and closed his eyes. "That stone was the Dragonsbane. The Wizards of the City quickly discovered the powers of the stone, some of which you have seen. But the greatest power was that of summoning dragons. The King who held the stone could order any dragon to do his bidding – and the dragon would have to obey."

"Right!" said the Harp. "Even if you told it to do a tap dance on a volcano or go swimming with lead armbands." Rose glared at it.

"So the Dragonsbane was set into the sceptre of the Kings of Dun Indewood and became its greatest treasure. No dragon dared come against the City while the stone remained in the hands of the Kings. But then the line of Kings failed…"

"Failed!" crowed the Harp. "Hah! I'll say it failed! Those last Kings were as nutty as a bag of mixed fruit and nuts without the fruit."

The Runemaster glared at it. "Silence," he growled warningly.

The Harp ignored him. "The maddest of the lot was old King Madimus III. Ever hear about him? The old goofball thought he was made of feathers and could fly like a bird." The Harp cackled nastily. "He carried on believing that until the day he leapt off the highest tower of the castle."

"Will you be silent!" The Runemaster's voice was icy. The Harp ignored him and sang:

> "He flew through the air with the greatest of ease
> He swooped like a bird as it soars on the breeze
> But having no wings, in the end he went SPLAT!
> They found his remains all squashed up in his
>   hat…"

"His last words were: 'Aaaaaaaargghhhhhh!'" The Harp gave a guffaw, which ended in a stifled gurgle as the Runemaster seized the obnoxious instrument and twisted it till its frame creaked. "All right, all right," said the Harp in sulky tones.

The Runemaster placed the Harp back on the table. Its voice took on an injured whine. "I'm just trying to give these people a bit of historical background, do you mind? The old foo— the old King," it corrected itself, catching the Runemaster's warning glance, "died childless and messily. The people of Dun Indewood decided that they'd had enough of gonzo Kings and took the opportunity to rid themselves of the monarchy. In its place they created the office of High Lords."

After a moment's pause, the Runemaster took over the story, "And so there were no more Kings: but still no dragons came. The powers of the stone were forgotten. It became simply one more item in the City treasury.

"Then, on the night that Gordin Mandrake became the High Lord, the Dragonsbane vanished. It was said that a thief had stolen it. My master at that time and my predecessor as Chief Wizard of Dun Indewood, Tarkwin the Wise, set off in search of the stone. That is the tale that I was told when I first came to the citadel." The old man paused, then said heavily, "It was a lie."

Will looked puzzled. "You mean, the Dragonsbane wasn't stolen…?"

"Oh, yes, it was stolen – but by Tarkwin himself. The scroll Humfrey brought me just now is his death-warrant, signed in secret by Lord Gordin in case Tarkwin should come into his hands."

The Harp gave a snide chuckle. "So Tarkwin the Wise became Tarkwin the Light-Fingered."

The Runemaster shook his head sadly. "He must have taken it to learn its deepest secrets and make himself more powerful still – but he never did. Somewhere in the wastes of the Dark Forest, he met a dragon." The Runemaster paused, as if considering what to say next. After a moment, he shrugged and said only: "The stone passed back into the possession of our enemies."

The old man leaned back wearily. "When I set off in search of the Dragonsbane, I thought I was doing penance for my old master's failure. I never imagined I was making amends for his crime. At last, I found the stone in the possession of the Dragon of the Ragged Mountain."

The Runemaster's face looked more lined and careworn than ever. "How I prevailed and carried away the Dragonsbane, I shall not say. Now I have brought the stone back to the City and the City no longer wants it."

The Harp gave a mocking sigh. "That's showbiz! One day you're hot, the next, you're not."

"When I got back to the City," the old man continued, "I cast the runes. Imagine my horror at what they foretold! My return with the Dragonsbane had actually increased the danger; and the City's only hope was..."

"A clodhopping beanpole who was stupid enough to take the rap for Lord Greasychops," finished the Harp. It stared pointedly at Will.

The Runemaster gave it a quelling look. "I had been away from the City for many years. In any case, the runes indicated that the person I sought lived outside the City..."

Rose took up the story. "So the Runemaster came to see me – well, my Grandmama actually. She's a witch, you see..."

"A good witch, of course," said the Harp with an unpleasant leer, "not the sort that lures little children into gingerbread houses and sticks them in the oven. At least, not so's they could ever prove it..."

"Shut up," Rose told it. The Harp was silent. "Grandmama knows everyone who lives in this part of the Forest," she went on, "but she couldn't think of anyone who fitted the prophecy. So the Runemaster asked me to keep my eyes and ears open for any strangers in the Forest." She gave Will a perky grin. "Then you showed up. You didn't live in the City or the Forest; and the runes' description fitted you like a pair of made-to-measure tights."

"Sho the Runemashter made sure you went to Knyght School," said Humfrey, "and he hired me to keep an eye on you. I shtaked out the school from the old tower and Luigi brought me pizshash."

The Harp rolled its wooden eyes. "He means pizzas. Will someone wipe the spit off me, please?"

Humfrey gave the instrument a malevolent look. "Anyhow, it don't take no abacush to figure that whatever the danger ish, it'sh got to do with the shtone."

"Humfrey is right." The Runemaster nodded slowly.

"The Dragonsbane arrives back in Dun Indewood just as the City is about to be thrown into mortal danger. The two must be linked."

Will looked thoughtful. "I suppose it could be a coincidence."

Humfrey snorted. "When you been around ash long ash I have, you shtop believing in coinshidenshesh."

Much later, when Rose and Humfrey had gone and the fire had burned to ash, the Runemaster, who had been silent and deep in thought for some time, looked up at Will.

"Wouldst like to see a dragon?" he asked quietly.

Will, who had been drowsing by the still-warm hearth, became instantly alert. His eyes shone. "A dragon?"

The Runemaster took the Dragonsbane and placed it in his wine goblet, in the centre of the table, so that it looked like an outsize egg sitting in a too-small cup. Then he beckoned to Will.

"This undertaking is not without danger," he warned softly. "The Dragonsbane has many powers, but it is a perilous tool. In order to make use of it, thou must give thyself up to it." Will gave him an inquiring glance. "Thou and I must touch the stone and project our life force into it. While we gaze therein, the life will leave our bodies. They will remain still and cold, unbreathing, unmoving, unchanging until we return."

Will gulped. "What if something happens to the stone, while we're inside it?"

The Runemaster looked grave. "Then we would be trapped. Thou must not break contact with the stone or thy life force will be separated from thy body, perhaps forever. Art thou still prepared to undertake this adventure?"

Will nodded.

"Then gaze into the stone. Look beneath the surface. Look beyond what is, to what may be."

Will stared at the stone. He gazed at the cloudy, milky surface, trying not to blink, until his eyes began to cross and his head to ache. "I can't see anything," he started to complain – and broke off as, suddenly, he could.

Will found himself looking at a strange scene. He seemed to be inside a vast cave. Looking around – Will gasped in astonishment and awe – he saw dragons, many dragons. Each lay asleep, curled around a pile of gold and precious jewels.

Will caught his breath as his view changed suddenly, as if his head had suddenly shot up into the air.

A voice spoke inside his head. *Who art thou, manling?* It demanded. *What dost thou in my mind?*

Will was confused for a moment, but then a flood of joy and awe swept over him as he understood. He was inside the mind of a dragon!

Chapter Fourteen

Of Will's encounter with the Dragons of the Dark Forest, and how the Harp of the Kings asked for a Right Good Kicking.

Will tried to speak, and realised he couldn't. His own body was still in the citadel, gazing into the Dragonsbane. He would have to try and project his thoughts to the dragon.

My name is Will… he thought.

Begone! The dragon's voice was sharp with irritation. **Thou hast no business with me!**

The boy is my apprentice. The Runemaster cut in sharply. *He is protected by the power of the Dragonsbane. Thou must answer him and obey him.*

Two of thee! the dragon hissed in fury. It sighed and subsided. **What is thy will?**

Will gazed around the strange scene. He had a thousand questions burning to be asked, but it was hard to put even one of them into words. At length, he began: *What is your name?*

My name in the language of Dragons is M'uat'ovanu An Tinotherran. You may call me Brightscale.

At Will's unspoken urging, the dragon looked around the cave. *Why are there so many dragons here?* Will asked. *I thought dragons lived alone, to guard their hoards.*

A roar of harsh, draconic laughter echoed through Will's mind. **What would be the point of that? A dragon's hoard is its pride and its glory. Why should it hide it away as if ashamed? If thou hast it,** Brightscale drawled, **flaunt it.**

The other dragons were by now waking up and stretching their great bat-like wings. One by one they leapt into the air and flew towards a wide opening high in the cave. Will, following their flight, looked up into it and saw stars.

Follow them! he ordered impulsively. *I want to see them fly.*

As thou commandest, said the dragon sardonically; but it leapt into the air with a powerful beat of its wings and surged towards the mouth of the cave.

Brightscale landed on the lip of the cave entrance. For a moment, Will watched entranced as the dragons wheeled and circled in the air, moonlight flashing on their scales. Then Brightscale gathered himself and leapt, and Will gave himself wholly to the joy of the dragon's flight.

The dragon swooped low over the Dark Forest. A flight of roosting pigeons scattered in panic as the huge shadow loomed over them. Then the dragon began to climb with slow beats of its powerful wings, rising away from the treetops.

Through the dragon's eyes, Will gazed down at the treescape. *Where are we?* he wondered. *I mean,* he added hurriedly, *how far are we from the City?*

I know not. The dragon spoke casually. **The Forest is so great and thy manling City is so small. Tell me where thy City is,** it went on cunningly, **and I shall tell thee how far off it lies.**

He does not know. The Runemaster's voice cut in again. *And if he did, he would not tell thee, lest thou take it into thy head to attack his home and burn it to the ground.*

The dragon shook its great head dismissively. **We have no interest in the doings of Men. We stole their gold, when they had it. Now...** The dragon gave a contemptuous snort. **Men do not matter to us. They have nothing that we need.**

Except the Dragonsbane, said the Runemaster coldly.

Will was looking down at a clearing in the Forest where a fire seemed to be burning. *What's happening down there?*

Without answering, Brightscale swooped down and circled a clearing where four dragons sat on their haunches. One of them held the branch of a tree on which was impaled the body of a great stag. One by one, the other three opened their massive jaws and shot a fierce jet of flame at the carcass, which the first turned on its spit so that each side should be roasted evenly.

Barbecue, explained the dragon briefly, and rose again.

Can you do that? asked Will excitedly. *Breathe fire, I mean?*

Of course. The dragon was affronted.

Will felt the dragon's body expand as it took a deep breath. It opened its mouth wide and sent a roaring jet of flame shooting across the night sky. All around flames banished the surrounding darkness as other dragons returned the fiery salute.

For a while, Will remained silent, glorying in the dragon's power; the rush of air over its vast wings, the moonlit Forest beneath. Then he remembered what the Runemaster had said about the Dragonsbane.

Brightscale, do you know the Dragon of the Ragged Mountain? He asked casually.

The dragon considered. *That would be the one called Greywing.* Its voice was disapproving. *He is an outcast. He went away. We do not know where. We do not care to know.*

Will was intrigued. *An outcast? Why, what did he do?*

It is not for thee to know what crimes a dragon may commit against its kind, said Brightscale stiffly.

He stole from another dragon's hoard, said the Runemaster. Brightscale hissed. *Did he not?* The Runemaster's voice insisted.

Yes, yes! The dragon's voice was tetchy. *If thou wilt have it so.*

Stealing from another's hoard is almost the only crime among dragons, Will, the Runemaster explained. *You must understand this, if you want to understand dragons. Think of it this way. I offered the Dragonsbane to the Council of the City. If they had accepted, who would it have belonged to?*

Well, Will thought slowly. *The City, I suppose – I mean, everyone.*

Exactly. The Runemaster sounded pleased. *But dragons don't think like that. If they had the Dragonsbane, it would belong to one single dragon; and all the other dragons would be its slaves. They do not want us to have the Dragonsbane, but they do not want one of their own kind to have it either.*

Brightscale swooped up to a ledge on the cliff below the mouth of its cave. ***I am weary***, it said sulkily. ***I would rest***.

Then do so, said the Runemaster. *Sleep, if thou wilt. We will watch with your eyes awhile.*

If thou must, the dragon said in bored tones. Its breathing slowed. It settled more comfortably on the ledge. Its voice faded into sleepy mutterings and then died away altogether.

But late into the night, through its great brooding eyes, Will and the Runemaster watched the dragons of the Dark Forest gliding, swooping, spinning and dancing in the moonlight air above the rippling trees on their great leathern wings.

A few days later, Will climbed the stairs of the citadel. He still had no idea what form his Quest was to take. The Runemaster had cast the runes several times, to no avail, and Will was beginning to feel discouraged. He wished something would happen. As he reached the top of the stairs, he heard raised voices coming from the Runemaster's chamber.

"So where am I now – in a nice, comfortable, warm room down in the castle, like you promised? No, I'm stuck up here in this damp, draughty ruin, catching my death of woodworm. And why? Because you couldn't organise a bad smell in a pigsty."

"Silence, thou wretch." The Runemaster's voice was harsh.

"Just because you can predict the future, you think you know everything." The Harp's sarcastic, whining voice echoed through the deserted halls of the ancient building. "Well, let me tell you, I've met tea leaves who can see into the future better than you."

"Thou goest too far!"

"I told you they'd never go for it, but did you listen? Oh, no! You knew best, as usual. As soon as you showed them the Dragonsbane, they were all supposed to say, 'Wow, thanks, great Runemaster. We have seen the light and we're going to mend our ways, and incidentally, how do you feel about being our new High Lord? And maybe a few statues, nothing too gaudy…'"

Will entered the chamber and found the Runemaster with his back to the Harp and his fingers in his ears. "That is a foul lie! I have never sought personal glory."

"Sez you!" sneered the Harp.

"Enough!" The Runemaster strode over to the hearth

and picked up the axe Will used for chopping firewood. He turned on the vexatious instrument. "You've been on my back for forty-five years..."

"Don't I know it! You've got really bony shoulders, do you know that?"

"I meant, thou hast been getting on my nerves for nearly half a century." The Runemaster swished the axe experimentally. "I think that's long enough."

The Harp's strings jangled nervously. "Don't do anything you might regret," it shrilled.

The Runemaster gave a strangled half-laugh. "Believe me, thou cacophonous creature, I will not regret this one jot."

"Well, don't do anything I might regret, then." Will stared aghast as the Runemaster raised the axe.

"Allow me one last song," pleaded the Harp. "Every condemned Harp should be granted a last request."

The Runemaster paused. "Very well, one last song."

The Harp strummed a sad little tune, and in a plaintive voice began to sing:

"Oh list, while I sing of a...

MAD, EVIL-MINDED OLD SCREWBALL; HE'S GOT AN AXE!" The Harp's panic-stricken shrieks twanged through the citadel. "HELP! HE'S CRAZY! MURDER!"

With a snarl, the Runemaster raised the axe above his head.

"Don't!"

The old man froze. Will rushed across the room and

snatched the Harp out of danger.

"Think about what you're doing!" pleaded Will. "This is the Harp of the Kings. It's magical! Unique!"

The Harp hummed enthusiastically. "You tell him, boy!"

"Even if it is a complete pain in the neck."

"Hey!"

The Runemaster pointed the axe at the offending instrument. "I have had enough of its insults and whinings."

"Look, I'll take it out of here. All right?" Will snatched up the Harp's travelling bag and backed carefully towards the door. "I'll take it right away, where you can't hear it. You can decide what to do with it later. All right?" he said again.

The Runemaster looked suddenly old and tired. He dropped the axe, nodded briefly at Will, and turned away. Will hurriedly crammed the Harp into its bag and raced down the steps and out of the citadel.

"Thanks for sticking up for me in there." The Harp's voice was muffled inside its bag. "I owe you one. Like you said, there's only one Talking Harp in this Forest. Mind you, I did know a talking drum, once, but he was a bit of a headbanger…"

Will opened the mouth of the bag and clapped one hand across the Harp's strings. It buzzed angrily.

"Shut up," Will told it. "I only rescued you because I knew if he chopped you up he'd feel terrible about it later. But I wouldn't."

Will looked the Harp straight in its carved, wooden

eye. "Now listen carefully. While you're with me, you can sing, but you can't talk. Deal?"

"You cannot be serious! Why should I...?"

"Do you want *me* to chop you up?" A nasty thought occurred to Will. Putting his lips very close to the Harp's carved ears, he said, "Or do you want me to give you to Rose?"

The Harp jangled as its strings shook. "The screwy dame? You wouldn't do that!"

"Try me."

"You are one seriously sick individual." But the Harp looked cowed.

"Good. And remember – no talking."

CHAPTER FIFTEEN

H ow Will Ignored the Harp's Warnings
and the Runemaster was Put on Ice.

W ill stood in the castle courtyard wondering where he could take the Harp where it wouldn't be a nuisance. He couldn't think of many places that qualified. A few minutes of listening to the Harp was enough to make most people want to run amok with an axe. Will certainly didn't fancy bumping into Symon and his cronies. Their sneers at finding him with a talking Harp would be bad enough; when the Harp started calling them names, they'd probably tear him to pieces.

"Hey, ugly! Are you planning to keep me smothered in this sack all night?"

"I told you, no talking!" ordered Will, looking around to make sure no one was about. "Be quiet."

That was it! Quiet – the library! Symon and his friends never went in there. Ignoring the Harp's muffled insults, Will hoisted the bag over his shoulder and headed towards the Knyght School.

He crossed the courtyard, entered the school and crept carefully through the corridors in an attempt to avoid the other students.

The Harp was still complaining. "How much further?"

"Pipe down, or I'll tighten your strings until they snap!"

"Calm down. We're not at home to Mister Temper."

Will tiptoed past the Recreation Room, where his fellow students were settling down to an evening of cards and board games. Groans of annoyance and yells of triumph floated out into the corridor and fragments of conversation drifted to his ears:

"Now, for a green slice, is the world: a) round; b) flat; or c) entirely covered by trees...?"

"Ooh! Ooh!" squeaked Symon's voice, "I know this one, don't tell me..."

"I'll swap you Dan Dann the Nightsoil Man for Mrs Thumbscrews the Executioner's Wife..."

"That's a six, so I go up this ladder and I get another go... that's a three, so – oh no!"

"Ha ha! Right back down the dragon to the start. Serves you right."

"Let's see what this card says – oh, great! 'Go to the dungeon, go directly to the dungeon, do not pass GO, do not collect 200 florins…"

"Time's up! The answer is: c) entirely covered by trees."

"I knew that!" Symon's voice was raised in complaint. "You didn't give me long enough…"

Will turned a corner and the voices faded into silence. He headed to the Great Staircase, which was lined with portraits of previous headmasters, all looking disapproving and constipated. Will bounded up the polished stairs to the top landing. Moving quickly along it, he came to a large, dark oak door. Giving a warning squeeze to the Harp in its bag, he opened the door and stepped in.

The library of the Knyght School was the greatest (and, indeed, the only) library in all of Dun Indewood. Shelves upon shelves of leather-bound volumes lined the walls. The smell was less impressive. Odours of musty parchment, mouldering leather and acrid dust filled the air.

In the fusty centre of the bookshelves (and the smells) sat the Master of the Records and Keeper of the Books. Master deLivre was a small, stooped figure with the pasty complexion of someone who didn't get out in the sun often enough. Whenever he moved, he rustled like the turning of old pages. He looked up as Will entered the library.

"What are you doing in here?" he snapped.

"Er… I wanted a book."

Master deLivre's cheek twitched. "Why?"

"To read?" suggested Will.

The Master of the Records and Keeper of the Books shook his head irritably. Most students of the Knyght School rarely ventured into the library. Consequently, they didn't bother Master deLivre, who held the opinion that his library would be a better place without people coming in, subverting his systems and ruining his records by taking books off the shelves where they belonged.

"If you must. Find a book and sit with the other boy, where I can keep an eye on you."

He pointed across the room to a curly mop of hair sticking out from behind a large book. Will recognised its owner straightaway.

"Gyles!" he called.

"You will be quiet in here!" ordered Master deLivre. "And don't leave any grubby fingermarks on the books or else…"

Will went over to Gyles, who was reading *Elephants, Red Herryngs and other Mythical Beasts*. He dumped the bag with the Harp in it on a vacant chair and gave his schoolmate a friendly grin. "I didn't expect to see you up here," he whispered.

Gyles sighed. "Every time I go to the games room, Symon makes me play *Snap!* for money and I always lose."

Will's forehead wrinkled. He didn't know anyone who was slower on the uptake than Symon.

"Why?" he asked.

"Because Jervaise always deals and he shows Symon

the cards before he shows them to me. Anyway, you try yelling 'SNAP!' through a gag."

Will gave Gyles a sympathetic pat on the shoulder and went over to the shelves to examine the books. For the next hour he waded though *Ye Bumpere Booke of Tales of Knyghtly Valoure* and *Ye Readere's Digeste Booke of Nastie Beasties*. Then he moved on to *Ye Historie of Ye Kynges of Dun Indewood*, in order to fill in the gaps in the royal history that the Runemaster had left. It was an illuminating experience.

"Listen to this," he whispered to Gyles. He read, "*The Kynges of Dun Indewoode dyed aftere thys fashion: Kynge Chols the Clumsy: was smotherede while huntynge moles. Kynge Bernud the Shortsighted: tried to kisse a Beare, thynking yt was the Queene in a fur coate. Kynge Kevyn the Unsavoury...*" Will's eyes widened. "Well, you don't want to know what *he* died of." He turned a shocked face to Gyles. "I thought Kings who didn't fall gloriously in battle lived long and wholesome lives, dying at a ripe old age, surrounded by their loved ones and mourned by the City."

Gyles shook his head glumly. "Most of them ended up like King Sedric the Unwary."

"What happened to him?"

"He died of generosity."

"People don't die of generosity."

"They do if they give their son and heir a *Little Poisoner Chemistrey Sette* for his birthday."

Will put aside *Ye Historie of Ye Kynges of Dun Indewood* and picked up its companion volume, *Ye Historie of Ye High*

Lordes. A few moments' reading were enough to convince him that the rule of the High Lords was much like that of the Kynges, only with more corruption. It was said that the High Lords were more wise, just and honourable than the Kynges had ever been. However, mostly this was said by the High Lords. For ordinary people, the main differences were that their taxes went up and the best jobs in the City seemed to go to members of the High Lord's family.

"Psst."

Will looked up from the book and raised an eyebrow at Giles. "Yes?"

Gyles returned the look blankly. "What?"

"I thought you said something."

Gyles shook his head and pointed to the "No Talking" sign.

"Psst."

Will suddenly realised where the sound was coming from. He thrust the bag on the floor and ducked under the table "Shut up! We're in the library," he hissed.

"There's a problem," the Harp told him.

"I said no talking."

"A big problem. Take me out and I'll tell you."

Gyles' face appeared under the table. "Why are you talking to your bag?" he asked in a worried voice.

Will grabbed the bag and straightened up. "No reason," he breezed. "Got to go. Bye…"

Will hurried out of the library looking for somewhere he wouldn't be seen or heard. He slipped into an empty classroom and pulled the Harp from its bag.

"Do you know how claustrophobic it gets in there?" moaned the Harp. "I'm a sensitive instrument. You can't treat me like this. I'm very highly strung."

Will shook the Harp until its strings hummed. "I told you, no talking!"

"But there's something very..."

Will raised a warning finger. "Ah!"

"But it's really..."

"Ah!"

"Oh, for crying out loud!" The Harp rolled its eyes. "OK, OK, I'll sing it for you!" It strummed an urgent little tune, and began to warble:

"D is for the dagger, that strikes with might and main,
A is for the agony that makes you scream with pain.
N is for the entrails, that flop out on the floor,
G is for the groaning as you welter in your gore
   (Have you got it yet? No? OK...)
E is for the eyeballs as they open wide in shock
R is for the ruffian who belts you with a rock.
   (Don't they teach you spelling at this dump of a
   school?)
Put them all together, they spell D A N G E R..."

Will's mouth dropped open. "Are you trying to tell me that someone's in danger?"

The Harp emitted a sound that was the musical equivalent of a slap on a forehead. "Amazing! Fantastic! Give the kid a coconut..."

"Who?"

"The man with the cloak and the attitude problem."

"You mean the Runemaster?"

"Two in a row! One more gets you the cuddly toy!"

"How do you know?"

"I spent over forty years with the old crock!" screeched the Harp. "Call it a gift – call it intuition – paint it pink and call it a radish, *I just know, OK?!*"

"Well, where is he?"

"Back in the citadel, you lunkhead." The Harp jangled impatiently. "Where we left him, dodo. Is that enough information? Or would you like me to sing it for you? *Don't wait or we'll be too late*... Hey, nice rhyme." Will stuffed it back into its bag. "I'll work on that."

The courtyard was bathed with moonlight as Will sped back to the citadel. He raced past the stone dragons and charged up the steps, the Harp in its bag banging against his backbone.

"Ooh! Agh! Ooya!" squeaked the Harp. "Hey, skinny ribs! Could you go a bit slower? Or wear a padded jacket? Or put on weight?"

Will ignored the wails of protest. Breathing hard, he reached the top chamber. Moonlight streamed in through the holes in the roof and walls.

"Runemaster!" Will called out. "Are you there?"

"Just yell 'No' if you're not!" sneered the Harp.

Will stepped forward carefully – and gave a cry of horror. Table and chairs lay overturned. Luigi's sun umbrella was rolling from side to side on the stone floor. The tapestries hung in shreds.

And spread-eagled in the middle of it all was the Runemaster.

Will stooped over the motionless form, tears springing to his eyes. "He's dead," he whispered.

"I don't think so." The Harp's voice was harsh with annoyance. "Get me out of this bag!" it ordered. Trembling with shock, Will complied.

The Harp glared at the prostrate figure. "Hello!" it screeched. "Mr Runemaster, wakey, wakey! This is your morning call. WAKE UP!"

"Ssh! You're making enough noise to waken the dead," hissed Will.

"Ding! The boy's going for the big prize."

"What's wrong with him?"

The Runemaster remained inert on the floor. The Harp let out a sigh. "He's been using the Dragonsbane," it concluded.

Will gave it a horrified glance. "We've got to get him back!" He began to shake the Runemaster.

"Shaking him won't do any good. Hey, what am I saying?" The Harp's voice dripped with malice. "Go ahead, shake away. Give him a kick for me!"

"Will that help?"

"No," admitted the Harp reluctantly. "We can't get him

back because the Dragonsbane's gone."

Will looked around wildly. "Gone?"

"Can you see it around here? You think maybe it just went for a stroll?" The Harp shook its carved wooden head. "His life force is inside the stone. Whoever's taken the stone has got the Runemaster."

In mounting panic, Will made a frantic but fruitless search of the chambers. The Harp was right, the Dragonsbane was nowhere to be found.

A feeling of helplessness washed through Will. "I'll go and get Humfrey or try to find Rose; they'll know what to do." But before he could act on his decision, there was a clattering of metal at the door.

"Uh-oh," said Will softly, "I think we're in trouble."

The Harp gave him a nasty grin. "What do you mean, 'we'? I'm a musical instrument, kiddo. Nobody's going to accuse yours truly of putting the old man's lights out."

Will stood transfixed as the door burst open and a dozen helmeted guards spilled into the room. They stared stony faced at Will as he stood over the lifeless body of the Runemaster.

"It's not what you think..." Will began. But the explanation died on his lips. He gave a gasp of horror as Symon stepped out from the throng of guards. His face was a mask of malevolent glee as he pointed at Will.

"Pig boy, you have killed the Runemaster." Symon turned to the guards. "He is a murderer. Arrest him!"

Chapter Sixteen

How Will stood accused of Murder and had to Scarper Most Speedily, and what he said to an Evergreen Shrub.

"So, you murderous, monstrous, malodorous mound of maleficence," spat Sir Regynild, "at last, you have shówn yourself in your true colours!"

The guards stood around Will in an unfriendly circle. Symon had called his father to the citadel and Gordin had summoned the staff of the Knyght School. They all stood around Will as he knelt, at swordpoint, on the cold stone floor.

Sir Regynild's voice was gloating. "You will be flogged by every member of staff in turn, until your craven, cringing carcass begs brokenly for death…"

Lord Gordin seemed barely in control of himself. His skin had an unhealthy, greenish tinge and his limbs trembled. But his voice was as harsh and powerful as ever. "And then," he rasped, "whatever remains will be thrown into the deepest, darkest, most rat-infested dungeon of the castle, to lie there until it rots."

"Sir... My Lord!" Will struggled to raise his head. "I swear I did no harm to the Runemaster."

"The word of a pig boy!" mocked Symon.

"In any case, I couldn't have attacked him. I was in the library all evening," Will protested. "Ask Gyles le Cure Hardy. He'll tell you."

Gordin grunted and nodded to a guard. A few minutes later, Gyles was hustled in, rubbing his eyes and looking thoroughly scared.

"Now listen to me, boy." Sir Regynild gave Gyles a quelling look. "This lying lumpfish claims that he was in the library with you this evening. Is that true?"

"Yes... Sir," Gyles quavered. "He was there." He looked up into the savage face of the Head, and the glittering, malevolent eyes of the High Lord, and his nerve failed him. "But he left." His face working, he pointed accusingly at Will. "You left the library, Will, you know you did!"

Will gave a hollow groan.

The High Lord nodded. "Take him away."

Every eye was on Will as a new voice cut through the air like a whiplash.

"OK! Don't nobody move!" The voice had a rasping quality to it. "I got a crossbow pointing right at Lord

Symon's back. Don't nobody turn round or the kid gets it!"

Lord Gordin began to turn his head.

"No, Dad!" Symon's voice was a squeal of terror. "He's not bluffing! Save me! Help!"

"Call the guards off or your son's a kebab." The voice was merciless. "I mean it."

"He means it, Dad!" Symon was blubbering with fear. "Oh, Mummy!"

Grudgingly, Gordin gestured. The guards let go of Will and stood back.

"Well? Get going, you great oaf!"

Staring in stunned disbelief at a point somewhere behind the trembling Symon, Will slowly backed away from his captors – then turned and fled.

"OK. Nobody move while I count to five. One... two... three... four... fourandahalf – *wait for it, wait for it*... five..."

When the guards and Lord Gordin turned, there was no one behind Symon; only the Harp, standing on a bench where Symon had left it, looking smug.

Gordin walked over to it and leaned forward. Quietly, he said: "You didn't say anything just now, did you?"

The Harp remained silent.

Gordin nodded and turned to his men. "As I thought, the Runemaster was using magic to throw his voice. The harp can't speak. It is merely a dumb instrument."

"Dumb instrument!" shrieked the Harp. "I got more brains than you, Ugly. Let me tell you..."

The Harp stopped suddenly, and gave a hollow groan. "Oh, rats!" it said.

Will scrabbled desperately at the locked City gate.

"Now, now, young Will." Rolph's slow voice echoed between the strong stone walls of the gatehouse. The guard stepped forward, his boots ringing on the cobbles. "You can't go out this time o'night, even if you 'ave forgot your pigs. Rules is rules."

Will grabbed the front of Rolph's jerkin. "Listen, Rolph," he gasped. "They're after me... Lord Gordin and all his guards..." He controlled himself with an effort. "They say I murdered the Runemaster. I didn't, he's not dead, but he will be if I don't get away and find someone to help him. Let me out, Rolph. Please."

Rolph stared at him, and shook his head in the slow way of the hard-of-thinking. "I dunno, Will. Rules is rules..."

Will slumped in despair.

"Rules is rules," Rolph repeated slowly," and what's right is right; but what's wrong is wrong, too." Will looked up with renewed hope. "They won't listen to you if they catch you; they'll chop you to bits first and ask questions afterwards." Rolph shook his head. "That's wrong."

He took the great iron key from his belt and turned it in the lock. He shot the bolts back and the gate creaked open. Will clasped Rolph's arm briefly in thanks and slipped out into the night.

Rolph locked the gate and was leaning against it whistling tunelessly when Will's pursuers came roaring down the narrow street.

Their leader clattered to a halt, breathing hard. "Have you seen a young lad come this way?"

Rolph's face was a study in innocence. "Young lad... young lad...? What, about so high?" he held his hand, palm downwards, at shoulder height. "Dark hair, green eyes, wearing Knyght School uniform, a bit crumpled?"

"Yes, yes! That's him!"

Rolph rubbed his chin slowly. Then he gave the guard captain a smile of deep stupidity. "Noooo... nooo... I ain't seen anyone like that..."

Unaware of this, Will raced on. As he went further and further from the City, the paths grew narrower, the trees stranger. His only thought was to put himself as far as possible from Gordin's pursuit. His headlong flight carried him deep into the Dark Forest.

In a small clearing was a large stone and on top of the stone lay a crystal coffin. Inside the coffin lay a young girl, apparently lifeless. Standing, sitting and kneeling around the coffin, in attitudes of grief and woe, were seven little men.

As they waited, the noise of a body crashing through the bushes came to their ears.

"Hark!" said one eagerly. "Perchance, 'tis a handsome…"

Will burst into the clearing, leapt over the coffin without breaking stride, and disappeared into the undergrowth on the far side.

"…Prince," finished the dwarf lamely.

"Young people today," complained another. "No time for anyone."

"Always in a hurry," agreed a third. "Rush, rush, rush."

The first dwarf nodded sadly. "Hi, ho," he sighed.

Will pushed on through dense fronds of bracken. The trees closed in behind him. Their flaking bark was covered with moss and growths of pale and poisonous-looking fungus. Overhead, their branches laced through each other until their leaves almost blotted out the sky, reducing the pale moonlight to a ghostly glimmer. Still, Will pressed on.

Further into the Forest the going grew harder. The undergrowth became thicker and more tangled. Unseen and probably terrible things rustled in the bushes. Eyes peered out of the darkness, unblinking eyes. Balked by a tangle of thorns, Will turned towards one pair that disappeared immediately – only to reappear, a few seconds later, somewhere else – if they were the same eyes at all.

Will set off again. In the darkness the eyes seemed to multiply. The rustling increased, as though the unseen watchers of the night were moving with him, dogging his footsteps. Briars and brambles caught at his feet and clothes, almost as if they were deliberately clutching at him as he pushed by. Before long, Will's tunic was badly torn, and bright red drops of blood, like tiny rubies, sprang up on his unprotected skin.

Trees loomed out of the darkness, their gnarled trunks twisted into a thousand grotesque and threatening shapes. Their branches blocked his way, their roots tripped him, their twigs clawed at him like grasping fingers. Eventually, Will crashed headlong into an overhanging branch and fell to the ground, with stars exploding before his eyes and a ringing in his ears.

Something said, "Ooooh! That has got to hurt!"

Will shook his head to clear it, and glanced around cautiously. "Who said that?"

There was a rustling noise. "I did," said the voice.

Will peered into the darkness. "And you are...?"

"Very well, thank you."

"No, I meant..." Will paused. "You're not a *tree*, are you?"

The voice laughed merrily. "Don't be silly. Everyone knows trees can't talk."

"Right," said Will, feeling very relieved. "Good."

"I'm a leaf." There was a chorus of titters and rustles. "Say hello, boys and girls," the voice continued.

"Hello!"

"Hello!"

"Hello!"

"Nice to meet you," said Will cautiously, feeling his head in case it was coming off.

"You'll have a nasty bruise there. I should go and put something on it, if I were you," said the voice sympathetically. "Feeling better now?"

"Er… yes, fine," said Will quickly. "Thanks," he added, remembering his manners. "I think I'll be going now."

There was silence after Will left the glade.

Then there came muffled sniggering, followed by a burst of laughter.

"Hey, lads! Lads!" The holly bush that had been talking to Will shook with mirth. "Did you hear that, lads? I told him that leaves can talk and the fool believed me! Terrific gag, eh, lads?"

"We heard, Noel," said a hawthorn bush wearily. "You're a riot."

The holly bristled. "Oh, get lost, spiky."

"Who are you calling spiky? You ought to show your elders some respect."

"That's right!" snapped a nearby elder.

"Deciduous shrubs," muttered the holly sulkily. "No sense of humour."

At length, Will could run no further and he collapsed in a panting heap. At least they won't dare follow me this far, he thought. I've outrun them. I'm safe!

"Well, hellooo again," came a deep voice right in his ear.

Will looked up and gave an agonised groan as he recognised its owner. "Not... you... again," he gasped.

The Highwaywolf grinned ferociously. "I'm afraid so," it said apologetically. "And, do you know, I'm feeling most frightfully hungry? So this time, I think we'll skip the chit-chat, if it's all the same to you, and just go straight into the savage tearing of flesh. Agonised squeals for mercy are optional." It licked its chops.

"Oh, why don't you push off."

The wolf blinked at Will. "I beg your pardon?"

"You heard me! I've had a bad day." Will's hand closed over a fallen branch. He grasped it and staggered to his feet facing the wolf. "You want a fight? You've got one!"

The wolf's air of urbanity evaporated. Its muzzle twisted into a snarl – and suddenly, it wasn't a big dog in a silly costume. It was a hungry, pitiless killer – and it was angry. Its hackles rose as it stalked towards Will on stiff legs, death in its eyes.

Will gripped the fallen branch tighter but the rotten wood crumbled in his hands. He watched in despair as the branch snapped in half under its own weight and thudded to the ground at his feet. Still, he didn't flinch. He waited for the wolf's attack with nothing but his bare hands.

"Naughty, naughty."

The wolf jerked convulsively at the sound of the new voice. Next moment, the ferocious beast had shrunk back into a cringing cur.

"Not again!" it whined.

Rose stepped into the clearing, crossbow at the ready. "What have I told you about eating people?" she said in the sort of sorrowful voice mothers reserve for children caught with their fingers in the biscuit tin.

With a frustrated snarl, the wolf turned from Will and plunged into the bushes. Firing from the hip, Rose set a crossbow quarrel hissing after its retreating form. A howl of pain indicated that the shot had found its target.

"Some creatures." Rose shook her head. "You try to be patient, you try to be kind, but in the end, the only thing they really understand is an arrow in the bum."

She gave Will a sweet smile. "Oh, it was nothing, you're welcome."

Will stared at her. "What?"

"Sorry, I thought you said 'Thank you'."

Will was still breathing hard. "I could have taken him."

"Of course you could," agreed Rose in her most infuriating voice.

"I had the situation under control," he insisted.

"Of course you did." Rose looked at Will quizzically. "What on earth are you doing out here, anyway?"

As Will told her, Rose's face betrayed her feelings at the news – shock, concern, and, as he came to the end of his story, furious anger. "And you *left* the Runemaster?" she demanded.

"I had half the City after me, baying for blood," Will pointed out hotly. "Yes, I left him. What would you have done?"

Rose ignored the question. "We've got to go back. We've got to save him."

"But he's all right," Will protested. "His mind's in the Dragonsbane, but his body will be fine if we can…"

Rose grabbed him by the arm. "His body *isn't* all right," she said fiercely. "He's cold, he's not breathing. What are they going to think?"

Will waved his hands in exasperation. "I already know what they think. They think he's dead," he snapped.

Rose nodded. "And what do they do with dead bodies in the City?"

Will started to reply, then felt himself go cold all over. In a faltering voice, he whispered: "They burn them."

CHAPTER SEVENTEEN

How Will became a Dame and returned
to the City in Cunning Disguise, and of
Humfrey's Inquestigations.

A few hours later, in the safety of Rose's cottage, Will
was complaining loudly. "I don't see why I have to wear
this," he moaned, as Rose forced a rough, green woollen
dress over his head and shoulders.

She tutted. "You want to go back into the City. I told you,
I'll go and see what's happening to the Runemaster..."

"And I stay here biting my nails while everything
happens somewhere else? No thanks."

"Well then, you'll need a disguise. Otherwise, Gordin's men
will nab you and that'll be that. End of Quest. End of story."

"I know that," wailed Will, "but why a dress? Why
can't I go disguised as an old man or even a sheep?" he

added, scratching at the coarse material.

"Stop moaning and breathe in," ordered Rose as she began to button up the dress. "I haven't got any old man's clothes and can you go 'baaaa'?"

"Buuuur," said Will.

"Pathetic. Anyway, Granny's dress was available."

"Won't she mind me wearing it?" asked Will.

"It had a wolf in it last year," said Rose darkly, "so I don't suppose she will. You're not as hairy, for one thing."

Will didn't know what to say to that so he shut up and wondered why he was letting Rose talk him into this. Rose's grandmama's dress was a bit frumpy and it smelled of mothballs. It wasn't his idea of what a Knyght should wear while undertaking a dangerous Quest.

Rose went over and opened a large wooden trunk by the hearth. Reaching in, she pulled out a hooded cape, a walking stick and a pair of thick, lumpy black stockings.

Will's heart sank further. "Granny's?"

Rose nodded and handed them over. Will gave a deep sigh of resignation and put them all on.

Rose looked him up and down and smiled. "There," she said, "Your own mother wouldn't know you."

"I hope not," said Will, "I really do."

The first rays of sunlight were just beginning to stretch and yawn their way over the tops of the Forest trees as Rose and

Will arrived at the West Gate of the City. Crowds of people milled around as they waited for Dun Indewood to open for the day. Peasants who farmed the scrubby land around the walls were driving their protesting animals to market. Sheep and pigs were getting mixed up, while their owners yelled and waved their arms about in useless attempts to keep them apart. Cows stood idly chewing the cud, and geese flapped about, hissing like kettles and pecking everybody in reach.

Finally, the City gates creaked slowly open and the crowd surged forward. Will's heart pounded as he noticed that there were more guards on duty than usual.

"Just look straight ahead," ordered Rose.

Bent almost double, with one hand clasped to the small of his back and the other gripping his walking stick, Will set off through the throng in an exaggerated hobble. "Oh, me poor old back," he mumbled in a high, croaky voice. "Oh, me poor old legs. Lackaday and mercy me," he added for good measure.

Rose slipped an arm round his shoulders. "You're supposed to be my grandmama," she hissed, "not the Wicked Witch of the Woods. Just act naturally. In that disguise, nobody will ever recognise you."

"Oi, old lady, come here!" A guard beckoned. Will's heart tried to hide behind his adam's apple.

"Stay calm," hissed Rose.

"I am calm. It's just my legs that are shaking." Will raised his voice. "Yes, young man?" he squeaked, pulling his face further into the depths of the hood as they approached the guard.

"Who are you and where are you going?"

"Mercy me and lackaday, dearie..." gibbered Will.

"She's just my old grandmama, going to market to buy provisions," interrupted Rose, stamping on Will's foot.

"Ow! Gerroff!" yelled Will. "Dearie," he added, a little late.

The guard eyed Will suspiciously before thrusting a piece of parchment into his face. "Have you seen this boy?" he barked.

Will stared at a hastily drawn, and not very flattering, picture of his own face. The words 'Wanted' and 'Large Reward' were prominent.

"Oooh, no, I don't think so, dearie."

The guard turned to Rose. "What about you?"

Rose gave the picture careful consideration before shaking her head. "No. I'd have remembered seeing someone that ugly."

Will gave Rose a fierce stare. "I thought he looked quite handsome. *Dearie*."

Rose gave Will's hand a consoling pat. "It's just your poor old eyes, Grandmama."

"Wait till I get you home, dearie," growled Will, clenching his fists.

The guard's eyes narrowed. "I reckon there's something fishy goin' on here..."

"What's up, Syrill?" Will gave an inward groan as the comfortable figure of Rolph waddled over. The old guard was sure to recognise him.

Rolph eyed Rose and her 'grandmama'. "That's all

right, Syrill," he said easily. "I knows this old gal. She's harmless. You can let her through."

Syrill looked sullen. "If you say so." Irritably, he waved Will and Rose through the gate. Will was overcome with relief. His disguise was actually working. It had even fooled Rolph!

"Morning, Willum." Will's illusions were dashed as Rolph fell into step beside him, taking his arm. "Listen," hissed the guard, looking around to make sure they couldn't be overheard, "make sure you keep away from the Street of a Quite a Lot of Potholes; there's a roadblock with enough of Lord Gordin's men there to start a war. They're armed to the teeth and all looking out for you."

Will nodded a thanks and hurried along into the relative safety of the City.

"Great disguise," he hissed up at Rose, "they'll never recognise me…"

"We got through, didn't we? Come on, let's go and find Luigi."

The small square was quiet as Rose and Will arrived at Luigi's restaurant. Rose knocked carefully on the door. A fit of barking was followed by a sleepy voice bellowing from an upstairs room. "Go 'way!"

Rose rapped more urgently. "Open up, Luigi! It's Rose."

"We's closed!"

Rose clenched her fists. "Do you want to open up this

minute?" she called as loudly as she dared. "Or do you want me to give your restaurant instant air conditioning by kicking all your doors and windows in?"

"All ri', all ri', I'm coming." There followed barking, shouts of "Be quiet", shuffling footsteps and scrabbling paws. At last, the door was thrown back. Luigi stood blinking in a rainbow-coloured nightshirt and nightcap that matched his dreadlocks. Hot Dog threw himself at Will and began fondly licking his cheek.

Luigi rubbed the sleep from his eyes. "Rose!" He glanced briefly at the caped figure before him. "'Ello, Will. Come in quick-like."

As they slipped into the restaurant, Will glowered at Rose. "Great disguise… even the dog recognises me!"

Rose and Will filled Luigi in on the previous night's events, while the pastafarian scowled and pursed his lips. "Hmm, is-a bad news." He looked thoughtful. "We need a plan. Rose, you go an' get Humfrey. Tell 'im to get 'ere tutti-fruiti and bring 'is bag of tricks."

"Why can't I go?" Will protested.

Luigi shook his head. "Is-a best you stay here. You don' wanna be meetin' up with Lord Gordin. I don' think you's exactly his Pasta of the Month right now."

Will gave a wordless cry as a bolt of realisation suddenly hit him.

Rose glared at him. "Don't screech like that. What's the matter with you?"

"Gordin! Of course! It had to be! It's so simple!" Will cried.

Rose and Luigi looked at him. "What are you talking about?"

"It's got to be Gordin," replied Will, wondering why he hadn't worked it out before. "He's the thief!"

"Gordin?" Luigi and Rose exchanged glances.

"Gordin's been scared of the Runemaster ever since the day of the Tournament," Will explained, waving his arms about in excitement. "I reckon he thinks the Runemaster has brought the Dragonsbane back to take away his power and rule the City himself. So he waited until the Runemaster was unprotected and inside the Dragonsbane, then he crept back into the citadel and took it! It's so obvious!"

"Obvioush, but wrong."

Rose spun round. "I was just coming to get you."

Humfrey stood in the doorway with a sack slung over his shoulder. "I know. I thought I'd shave you the bother." He raised a finger to his forehead, tapped it and pointed at Will. "Nice dresh, kid. Suitsh you." He frowned. "The hem'sh a little long – I'll take it up for ya."

Rose and Luigi sniggered. Will stared at Humfrey. "What do you mean, obvious but wrong?"

Humfrey threw the sack to the floor and started to pin up the hem of Will's dress. "Yep. The obvioush isn't alwaysh the anshwer, kid. You're letting emotionsh get in the way. If we're going to nail the bad guysh, we need to get all the factsh."

"But they're going to burn the Runemaster's body..." protested Will.

"Relax," said Humfrey, threading a needle with expert speed. "The old boy ain't goin' anywhere – not yet. It'sh a cushtom of Dun Indewood – high officialsh get to lie in shtate for a month and a day. The old guy'sh on a funeral bier in the Great Hall. I shaw him there, all shtretched out. No wonder they all think he'sh a shtiff."

Will looked blank. "A shtiff?"

"Yeah, a c-o-r-p-s-e: shtiff. He had guardsh and candlesh all around and everyone comin' in to pay their lasht reshpectsh."

Humfrey began to untie the sack. "I managed to shlip pasht the guardsh and do shome inqueshtigatin'."

Rose leaned forward. "In the citadel?"

Humfrey nodded.

"What did you find?"

"I had a lucky break." Humfrey smiled grimly. "The scene of the crime hadn't been dishturbed. Sho I had a look round for cluesh. Exhibit A."

He upended the sack and tipped out several pieces of broken wood and wire.

"The Harp of the Kings!" Will gasped. "It's been destroyed!"

Rose whistled. "It's gone to pieces all right."

"Itsh a gonner," agreed Humfrey. "Shomeone washn't happy with it."

"That narrows it down to everyone who knew it," muttered Rose.

Will stared disconsolately at the remains of the Harp. "But it's magical! It saved my life…"

"Oh, perlease," snapped Rose. "Don't start getting sentimental over a bit of wood and cat gut!"

Will ignored Rose. "Anyway," he said, "the thief didn't break the Harp. It was with me. Gordin must have smashed it for letting me go." He explained how the Harp had 'taken Symon hostage' and fooled the High Lord.

"And before that, it warned me that the Runemaster was in danger. It may know something that could help us. We've got to mend it."

Rose stared at the shattered instrument. "Good luck!"

Will turned to Humfrey. "Did you find anything else?"

The boggart nodded. "Shure, I did. I told you, I'm the besht. Did I ever tell you about the time I found the Green Eye of the Little Yellow God? He wash looking for that for agesh. Well, when I shay *looking* for it…"

"So what else have you found?" interrupted Will impatiently. "What makes you think the thief wasn't Gordin?"

"Becaushe all the evidence pointsh one way." Humfrey began to count off. "One: fire-scorched tapeshtry, two: shredded curtainsh; three: scratch marksh on the floor, clawlike, I'd shay; and four: Exhibit B." He reached into his jerkin and held up a flat, translucent, glass-like object. It was the size of a small hand and shimmered in the light. "Thish ish the clincher."

A memory stirred in Will's brain of a dream-like journey over the trees, and of gold and fire. He gazed at Humfrey's find, open-mouthed. "Is that…?"

Rose nodded. "It's a scale. The thief is a dragon."

CHAPTER EIGHTEEN

H ow Will was lumbered with a Quest and
What Followed at Grandmama's house.

L uigi smacked himself on the forehead. "'Oly
zabaglione! One of my customers was up at the castle las'
night an' he say he saw a dragon roamin' around in the
citadel."

Humfrey glowered at him. "You don't think you could
have mentioned thish earlier?"

"I didn' think nothing of it at the time," Luigi protested.
"The same customer tol' me las' week he found an
elephant in his wardrobe." He spread his hands. "Tha's
ridiculous-like. He's got a verra small wardrobe."

"Wait a minute." Will held his hand up for silence.
"The Runemaster told us that the last time the stone went

missing, it was the Dragon of the Ragged Mountain that had it."

"I was coming to that." Humfrey gave Will a withering look. "Call it a hunch, but I gotta gut feelin' the worm in the apple pie ish the aforementioned Big Lizard himshelf."

"Whew!" whistled Rose.

Will looked blank. "Is that bad?" he asked.

Rose and Humfrey nodded as one.

"How bad?"

"Well," said Rose carefully, "on a scale of one to ten, with one being 'Cuddly as a Snake' and ten being 'Diabolically Ferocious, Unspeakably Cruel, Breathtakingly Callous and Totally Without Mercy' – the Dragon of the Ragged Mountain scores about twenty-five."

Will gave a hollow groan. "Why does it have to be a ferocious dragon?" he complained. "Aren't there any nice domesticated ones?"

"Shure, kid. There are tame dragonsh like there are man-eating sheep."

"So, what are you going to do about it?" demanded Will.

"Me?" Humfrey stared at Will and raised an eyebrow. After several more seconds of pointed silence, Will realised that Rose and Luigi were also staring at him.

"What are *we* going to do?" Will hazarded.

More silence.

Will sighed. "What am *I* going to do?"

Rose looked earnestly at him. "The only way that you can prove that you're innocent is to find the Dragon of the Ragged Mountain, defeat it, recover the Dragonsbane, get back to Dun Indewood without being caught by Gordin's men, and restore the Runemaster to life."

There followed an even longer silence, which was eventually broken by Luigi. "Well tha's not so bad. Could be worse!"

Will gawped at him. "How could it be worse?"

The pastafarian shrugged. "You're right, it can't. I was just tryin' to cheer you up."

"So how do I go about finding this dragon?" asked Will resignedly.

"You don't," replied Rose tartly. "*I* do. You couldn't find your way to the privy with a map. Anyway, you wouldn't last a day out in the Forest on your own."

Will gave a small humph, but that was for public consumption only. Inside, he was pleased and relieved that Rose was going to be around. He didn't fancy dragon hunting on his own, even if it *was* what Knyghts were supposed to do.

Rose turned to Humfrey. "What about you?"

The boggart shook his head. "Someone'sh got to shtay here in Dun Indewood, to shee what Gordin'sh up to."

"Luigi?"

"You mus' be jokin'!" exclaimed the pastafarian. "Dragons is bad for your 'ealth. They bring you out in burns and death. Anyhows, I gotta restaurant to run, pizza to bake and customers to keep 'appy."

Rose gave Will a sardonic grin. "Just you and me, then." She slapped the table and stood up. "Well, Willum deSanglier, you wanted a Quest. You've just got one."

Rose rapped sharply on the door of Grandmama's cottage. "Come on, Grandmama, open up!" she yelled in exasperation.

"Not likely," came a snappish voice from inside. "You're not fooling me like that again."

Will's disguise had got him back out of the City. He and Rose had skirted round Swains Willingly, which was swarming with Gordin's guards. Will had insisted on calling at Grandmama's cottage after Rose had grudgingly admitted that the old witch might be able to mend the Harp: but getting invited in was proving to be a problem.

"It's me, Grandmama! It's Rose!"

"Pull the other one, it's got bells on." There was a pause, then Grandmama's voice went on in cunning tones, "Have you got any identification?"

Will grinned as Rose's jaw dropped open. "*What?*"

"A nice man from Help the Old Folks came round. He said I should never let anyone in unless they could prove who they were."

Rose spluttered. "I'm your granddaughter!" she managed at last.

"Oh, yes, I daresay. I've heard that one before, you know."

Will sniggered. Rose glared at him. Then, putting her lips close to the wood of the door, she said in a soft, syrupy voice, "I've got a basket of goodies."

The door opened a fraction. A beady, bird-like eye peeped out.

"Goodies?"

A few minutes later, Will and Rose were sitting round the kitchen table while Grandmama peered at the bits of Harp. "Hmmmph. Take more than a spot of glue to put this back together."

"You can do it, Grandmama," said Rose encouragingly.

"Listen, young lady, just because I'm a witch doesn't mean I can work miracles," the old woman snapped. She met Rose's eye and shrugged. "I've got a re-making charm lying about somewhere. Help yourself to scones."

She wandered away into the parlour. Will, who had been trying to nibble a rock-hard scone out of politeness, hastily wrapped it in his handkerchief.

Rose gave an impatient snort. "I still don't see why we need to fix that mouthy Harp."

"He might be able to help us find the dragon," Will argued. "Remember, he was with the Runemaster when he rescued the Dragonsbane."

"Here we are." Grandmama wandered back in carrying an ancient-looking leather book. She stared at Will who hastily took another scone. "Now, let's see:

Wing of bat and tongue of dog,
Tail of newt and legs of frog..."

She peered more closely at the book. "Oops, no, that's a cake recipe..."

Will put the scone down again.

"Where is it, where is it... hartshorn, harpies, Harps. Got it." She raised both hands above her head and chanted, *"Araldyte, Eevostycke, Sellotaype!"*

The room was filled with a sound like rushing wind and distant bells. Grandmama pointed at the Harp. Pale blue light flashed from her finger and surrounded the shattered pieces of instrument. Each piece began to glow with a coruscating halo of light. The sound increased, the light grew brighter. Cups and plates rattled on the dresser as fragments of wood flew together and joined seamlessly. Tangled strings unravelled and threaded themselves back into place.

There was a final burst of sound, a flash of light, and the Harp stood in the middle of the table, apparently none the worse for wear.

Grandmama cackled and blew a wisp of smoke from the end of her finger. "Yes, sir, I still got it..."

"Oh, rats!..."

A sudden cry from the Harp made Will jump. It began to shake and moan as if in the middle of some nightmare.

"Hey, can't you take a joke?... Did anyone ever tell you that you look beautiful when you're angry?... Hey, leave me alone! What are you?... Waargghh! OW!" The Harp's eyes shot wide-open and it stared around in panic. "Where am I? Who are you? More to the point, who am I?"

When it had calmed down, Will told the Harp everything that had happened since it had rescued him from Gordin's guards. "So," he concluded, "you warned me when we were in the library that the Runemaster was in danger. Did you see from who? Or what?"

The Harp groaned. "Listen, my frame aches, my strings are at breaking point, I've been battered and banged about." It closed its eyes. "I've got percussion. I can't remember a thing."

Rose leaned over the Harp. "Try harder."

It opened its eyes. "Uh oh, I remember you!"

"I'm flattered," replied Rose caustically.

"I wish I didn't."

"Listen, fatmouth," snapped Rose, "if it were up to me you'd be firewood. I don't want you on this Quest."

"What Quest?" asked the Harp.

Will smiled proudly. "We're heading into the Dark Forest to find the Dragon of the Ragged Mountain."

"TWANG!" The Harp gave a violent start. "We're going looking for dragons? In the Forest? You're crazy! You put me back together for this? Oh, thank you so much. Haven't you got any sense of self-preservation? Don't you remember the old song?"

"Which one?"

The Harp gave itself a good shake and burst out singing.

"*If you go into the Forest today, you're sure of a
    big surprise.
If you go into the Forest today, you'll probably lose
    your eyes.
'Cos every nightmare that ever there was,
Is bound to be there for certain because,
Today's the day they'll eat you for their picnic.
Picnic time for nasty things…*"

Will clamped his hand over the Harp's mouth and nodded to Rose, who opened the door.

Grandmama looked up. "Are you going out in the Forest *again*? Well, take a clean hankie, wrap up warm and don't go talking to any strange monsters."

"Yes, Granny," Rose said mechanically. Then she gave the old lady a pleading look. "Graaannnyyy…?"

Grandmama narrowed her eyes. "What do you want now?"

"Is that brag of yours still around?"

Will nudged her. "Brag?"

Rose elbowed him back. "Ssssh."

Grandmama shrugged. "That thing? Yes, for all the use it is. It's out back. Take it if you want. It's not worth the effort of the spell to keep it here. And it's eating me out of house and home…"

The old lady continued to grumble as Rose elbowed Will again. "Come on…"

Will stared at the creature in the small paddock behind Grandmama's house. "So that's a brag. What sort of a horse is it supposed to be anyway?"

Rose screwed her face up thoughtfully. "Well, it's not exactly a horse…"

"No kidding," said the Harp. "It's the horns… and the clawed feet… and the blazing red eyes. Dead giveaway."

"I suppose you'd call it a hobgoblin."

"A *what*?"

"A shape-shifter. It can look like anything it wants to, but mostly it likes to look like a horse. Sort of."

The brag skittered about in its paddock with a series of sideways leaps and bounds. Muscles rippled beneath its black coat. It gave Will a malicious grin.

Will folded his arms. "I'm not riding that."

"Me neither," snapped the Harp.

"It's perfectly safe."

"Of course *it's* safe," said the Harp caustically. "It's us I'm worried about."

Rose tutted. "I mean it's tame. It's just a night creature that likes causing mischief." The brag snickered and winked one wicked-looking red eye. "It tricked Grandmama into riding it once and chucked her in a pond. So she got mad and put a spell on it to make it visible in daylight. She uses it to pull her plough, but it's not very good at it. It's too skittish."

"You're telling me."

Rose ignored the Harp. "Look, Will, we don't have a choice. We'll never get to the Ragged Mountain on foot. We've got to ride."

"Well, what's wrong with horses?"

"For one thing, we haven't got any. And for another, the brag is faster. A lot faster. It's a magical creature and it's the only chance we've got of getting to the dragon and back in time to save the Runemaster. All right?"

Will sighed. "Oh, all right. You get up behind me."

Rose shook her head. "Oh, no. *You* get up behind *me*."

Will nodded helplessly. This Quest wasn't turning out quite as he'd imagined. Instead of carrying a lance and riding a white charger, he was carrying a lippy Harp and about to mount something that looked like a blacksmith's worst nightmare, riding pillion to a girl. What's more, he didn't feel excited and brave. He felt apprehensive, if not downright scared.

Rose clicked her tongue at the brag. "Come on, here, boy."

The creature ignored her.

"Come on, boy. Good boy. Here."

The brag continued to cavort around its paddock.

Will said thoughtfully, "I read that there are people called horse whisperers who talk to horses, very softly so that nobody else can hear, and make them do whatever they want."

"Is that right?" Rose climbed over the paddock fence and faced the brag. "Listen, you stupid beast!" she yelled at the top of her lungs. "If you don't stop messing about and do as you're told right now, you're cat food!"

The brag's head drooped. It trotted over to Rose and stood, nuzzling her shoulder in apology.

"Nice whispering," approved the Harp.

Rose led the brag out of the paddock and leapt on to its back. She reached down to take Will's hand. "Right, let's go."

CHAPTER NINETEEN

H ow Will suffered further Pain to his Backside and found that his Steed was nothing to Brag About.

"Waaaaaaaaaaaaaahhhhhhhhhhhhhhhhh!"

Rose looked over her shoulder at Will. "Stop moaning!"

"I'm not moaning, I'm screaming!" Will shut his eyes.

Rose had been right. The brag was faster than a horse. She hadn't mentioned how much faster. The Dark Forest was little more than a blur as they flew along. They weren't following a road, but the brag threaded its way between the trees with supernatural skill and appalling speed. Will opened his eyes again, just as a huge tree trunk appeared dead in their path; it was suddenly to the side, and then behind, before Will could even cry a warning.

"Relax," Rose told him. "The brag knows what it's doing."

"So do I! It's trying to kill us!"

When they finally halted that night, Will was so stiff from riding that he toppled off the brag and lay where he fell, immobile and groaning. Riding without a saddle was worse than Doctor Blud's beatings!

As the days passed, Will became more accustomed to the high-speed torture of riding the brag. Nevertheless, every evening he eased himself off the creature's back, moaning and rubbing himself where it was sore. He'd then eat a frugal meal of whatever the Forest could provide (mostly nuts and berries) before falling into an exhausted sleep.

Will had no idea how far they had travelled, or even whether they were moving in the right direction, but Rose seemed confident of their route. Every morning she would examine the ground carefully, then stand up, point and exclaim, "This way!"

Will was determined not to ask Rose how she knew – he didn't want to give her the chance to show off her superior knowledge of the ways of the Forest. However, his curiosity finally got the better of him.

"Do you work out which way to go from the position of the sun?" he asked one day.

"It depends," said Rose evasively.

"Or do you look at the moss and lichen growing on tree trunks or stones to work out where North is?"

"Maybe." The tips of Rose's ears began to turn pink.

"Or maybe she asks some highly tuned, but unappreciated instrument who's travelled this way before."

Rose pretended she hadn't heard the Harp's muffled voice.

The penny dropped. Will pointed an accusing finger at Rose. "You don't know where we are, do you?"

"Not exactly," she said defensively. "Do you?"

"I could work it out with an astrolabe!" said Will hotly. "If I could see the stars," he added in a subdued voice. "And if I had an astrolabe," he concluded lamely.

Rose rolled her eyes. "Come on. We've got a long way to go."

"I spy with my little eye, something beginning with T."

"Tree," said Rose instantly.

"Right. Your turn."

"I spy with my little eye, something beginning with L."

"Leaves."

As one day of travelling followed another, Will's apprehension gave way to boredom. Up to this point, every part of the Forest had looked like every other part. Just by looking around, Will was unable to tell that they had travelled anywhere at all. But in fact, they had covered many miles on the back of the swift, tireless brag; and according to the Harp, they were well on their way to the Ragged Mountain.

However, in places the Forest was too dense even for the brag. For several hours now, Rose and Will had been hacking their way through untrodden paths, overgrown with briars, thistles and bushes. Will's feet and arms ached.

"What kind of Quest is this?" he complained. "Nothing's happened to us since we set off."

"Good," said Rose grimly. "Let's hope it stays that way."

"It won't," said the Harp. Its voice sounded from the brag's saddlebag, singing:

> "With a tra la la and a hey nonny no,
> We're going to get our bits cut off!"

"There are some especially nasty Forest woodworm round here," Rose told it after the seventh chorus. "They can turn a fully grown oak tree into sawdust in four minutes. Would you like an introduction?"

The Harp took the hint and shut up.

Rose and Will travelled on. Broad-leaved Forest gave way to heathland full of gorse and bracken. They were forced to go many miles out of their way to avoid rivers. These could be forded quite easily; but Rose explained to Will that the brag was a magical creature that couldn't cross running water.

Now they began climbing into a range of hills covered with pine woods. The climb was arduous, and following an uncomfortable night in a clearing full of itchy pine-needles, tempers were frayed. Will and Rose had bickered constantly over breakfast, egged on by the Harp.

"Look, it's not fair!" Will glared at Rose. "I'm tired of riding behind you. You always get the front seat."

"Now you know how I feel!" chimed in the Harp.

"I can ride a horse too, you know."

"I keep telling you, this isn't a horse." Even Rose was beginning to look muddy and dishevelled, which didn't improve her mood. "You don't know anything about magical creatures. Anyway, you ride like a sack of potatoes."

The Harp cackled derisively.

"Is that so?" Will had had enough of Rose's superior attitude. "Let's see!"

He sprang to his feet and leapt on to the brag's back.

Rose's ill-tempered look changed to one of alarm. "Will, no!"

The brag, which hadn't been paying attention to the argument, reared in alarm at the unfamiliar grip on its back. Then it turned and looked Will straight in the face, giving him an utterly wicked, malicious grin.

Will reached down to take Rose's hand. "Come on…"

Next moment, the brag took off with Will clinging on

to its neck for dear life, yelling at it to stop. Even after they disappeared, its mocking, neighing laughter floated back through the trees.

Rose stared after it in dismay. The Harp snickered.

"Is there something you want to say?" she demanded.

"Nay," said the Harp. "I'm just a little hoarse."

"Shut up." Rose set her mouth in a grim line. She picked up the Harp, slung it over her shoulder and doggedly set off in the wake of Will and the wayward steed.

Several miles away, the brag raced on headlong through the trees. Twigs and needles, spindly and scratchy, whipped through Will's hair. The creature was going even faster than usual, bucking and leaping dangerously.

Just as Will was certain he was about to lose his grip, his mount shot through a gap and into a clearing. The carpet of discarded needles and cones gave way to coarse grasses, at the centre of which was a still, silent pool.

The brag gave a neigh of triumph and bucked out with irresistible power. Will sailed from its back and landed – SPLASH! – in the pond.

The brag capered on the bank, sniggering at him. Coughing and choking, Will doggy-paddled his way to the side of the pool and heaved himself on to the bank where he stood dripping.

"Look what you've done, you stupid creature!" Will shook his fist at the brag. "When I get my hands on you, I'll…"

Will was so busy telling the brag what he was going to

do to it that he didn't notice when the waters behind him parted. Long arms, spindly but horribly strong, reached out for him. The brag gave a mocking neigh and sped off.

Will felt a claw-like hand clutch his ankle. He spun round with a cry. The water was frothing and foaming and a hideous face with pale, staring eyes and needle-sharp teeth broke the surface of the pool. Gnarled hands grasped the folds of Will's tunic in an unshakeable grip and began to drag Will inexorably towards the dark waters.

Will gave a cry of terror and tried to break free. He had heard tales of the terrible water sprites that lurked in the dark, peaty pools of the Forest. These dreadful beings would wait for a Forest creature or lost traveller to come and drink. Then there would be a splash, a tortured scream – cut off in a second – and the unfortunate victim would never be seen again.

The sprite had dragged Will half into the pool. Its bloodless lips parted. In a creaking, bubbling voice, the foul creature spoke…

"Are you any good with drains?"

Taken aback, Will stopped struggling. "What?"

"Drains, my tadpole. They'm completely clogged. Sludge everywhere. Stagnant this water is, that's what. I've complained hundreds of times, but nobody does anything. Nobody cares about old Jenny Greenteeth."

"What a shame," said Will insincerely. "Do you think you could—"

"Well, my minnow, hows about newts? They'm all over the place. I've set traps, I've tried poison…"

"I don't know anything about newts, sorry…"

"How old d'you think I am?" The creature's breath, smelling of the mud at the bottom of ponds, made Will cough. "Go on, guess."

"Er… I don't know. Sixty years old?" Will guessed. "Seventy?"

The creature cackled. "I'm five hundred and eleventy-two. You wouldn't think it to look at me, would you?" Will gazed in horror at the creature's scaly, warty skin and said nothing. The sprite leered. "I've got all my own teeth, y'know."

Flinching at the rows of needle-sharp fangs, Will gabbled, "I'd never have guessed. Look, I'm afraid I don't know anything about drains, or newts, so do you think you could let me go?"

The sprite's pale tongue flickered wickedly. "What? A tastesome morsel like you? The plumpest, juiciest froglet old Jenny have seen in many a long year – let you go?" The creature cackled. "Oh, no, my little mayfly, you'm coming down to Jenny's larder."

Will hurled himself backwards. For a moment, the sprite's grip held firm – but then, the torn, threadbare material of Will's tunic ripped and he scrambled away from the deadly pool. With an unearthly screech of rage and frustration, Jenny Greenteeth sank back beneath the dark waters. A few sullen bubbles rose from the depths of the pool and spread ripples over its surface. Then there was silence and the pool lay as still and unruffled as though nothing had happened. Will sat on the bank, shivering from more than the cold.

CHAPTER TWENTY

How Death fell from the Trees and how Humfrey and Luigi learned of a Grave Development.

For the rest of that long day and the following night, Will stumbled through the Forest, trying to find his way back to Rose. He had no idea how far the brag had carried him – she was probably miles away. To begin with, he had tried calling, but had soon stopped when he realised his yells were more likely to attract something with a bad attitude and a big appetite.

He had lost all sense of direction. The Forest was dense and the sky cloudy. Neither sun nor moon appeared to guide him. The brag had completely disappeared and doubts came crowding into Will's exhausted mind. Was he going the right way? What should he do next? How long could he survive in the Forest on his own? For the first time, he was forced to admit to himself how thoroughly he relied on Rose and a cold hand seemed to clutch at his heart.

The pine forest gave way to mixed woodland as the path led downwards once more. The woods were dark, silent and watchful. Exhausted, Will tried to snatch a few moments' sleep in the broad fork of an ancient oak, but he had hardly closed his eyes when he heard a rustling through the undergrowth below. This was followed by a snuffling noise, which came nearer and nearer. Will held his breath. The thudding of his heart seemed to him to echo round the Forest.

The snuffling stopped. Will looked down.

Two enormous, luminous eyes stared up at him. From the unseen creature below came a long, blood-curdling, mournful howl. Will's blood froze in his veins. Then he heard voices, approaching through the Forest. Voices he knew very well.

"…it's your fault, for being so high and mighty…"

"It's your fault for getting on everybody's nerves…"

"You know-it-all nag!"

"You tuneless banjo!"

"Rose!" yelled Will. "Get away from here! There's something underneath this tree!"

Rose's voice floated up to him. "Of course there is. I wouldn't have found you without him. Here, Gally. Good dog."

The eyes disappeared.

"You can come down," Rose called. "He's perfectly harmless."

"Compared to the hoity-toity, music-hating grouch who brought him here," added the Harp in its usual caustic tones.

Will slithered down from the tree and stumbled towards Rose's voice. Something loomed beside her in the darkness; something huge and hairy and – a huge tongue slapped wetly against Will's face – licky.

"What is it?" he spluttered.

"A gally-trot. He'll be quite friendly to you if you're friendly to him, but if you run away he'll chase you. He's got an amazing sense of smell; that's how I managed to find you. I gave him the Harp's bag to sniff."

"Yeah, and did you bother taking me out of it first? I think not."

The gally-trot gave an urgent "woof".

"Yes, thanks, Gally." The huge dog trotted away. Rose turned back to Will. "He's a night creature and dawn is coming. He'll disappear at first light. Speaking of supernatural creatures, what happened to the brag?"

Will told her. Rose pursed her lips at the mention of Jenny Greenteeth.

"You were lucky," she told him. "If you'd met one of the really nasty water sprites like Nelly Longarms or Peg Powler, you wouldn't have got away so easily."

Will was thunderstruck. "Easily!"

"The real problem is that we've lost the brag."

"Hallelujah!" crowed the Harp. "No more getting thrown about and banged around…"

"I wouldn't be too happy if I were you." Rose looked

grim. "We're well on our way to the Ragged Mountain. Even on foot, we'll get there before they take the Runemaster for burning. But how do we get *back* in time?"

Will stared at her in horror. That thought hadn't occurred to him.

"Hah!" said the Harp. "We've still got to cross miles of trackless forest, reach the Ragged Mountain, find the hoard and get the Dragonsbane without being eaten by the dragon. I'd say, finding the way back is the least of our worries."

Will nodded. "We've got to carry on." He sighed. "Maybe Luigi and Humfrey will think of something."

"So whadda we do if Will and Rose don' come back before they barbecue the Runemaster?" asked Luigi.

"Haven't thought about it," replied Humfrey as he picked at a plate of pasta. "Been too busy makin' shure the old man'sh OK."

The boggart had been true to his word and kept a careful eye on the Runemaster. He'd visited him daily, sneaking into the Great Hall in a variety of disguises to avoid detection. He also picked up news from the street and by listening to the guards.

"What if they don' *ever* come back?" pondered Luigi darkly.

The boggart wagged a finger at the wavering pastafarian.

"You've gotta accshentuate the positive, eliminate the negative. My bonesh shay they'll be back in time. Now, pass the parmeshan."

But as the days dragged on and there was no news from Will and Rose, even Humfrey grew apprehensive.

"So whadda we do if they don' come back?" repeated Luigi for the umpteenth time.

The boggart shook his head grimly. "We watch them go and burn the Runemaster, and take shome shpare ribsh for the barbecue."

Will and Rose were now a long way from the City and the character of the Forest had changed again. The trees were less dense and the ground was a scorched, sandy colour, rather than the mulch-covered brown and black Will had become accustomed to. For the first time in days, Will felt the sun's warmth on his back.

"This is more like it," he said to Rose.

"Roar."

Rose held up her hand, ordering Will to stop. She glanced about, trying to spot the source of the noise.

"Roar."

It was coming from the trees above them.

"Look out – up there!" warned Rose.

Will jerked his head upwards and screamed as a golden blur came hurtling down at his head. It seemed as if the sun was falling on his head – except this sun had a large mouth filled with sharp teeth.

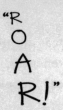

"R
O
A
R!"

"Move!" screamed Rose. She threw herself at him and the pair of them went spinning to the ground.

THUMP! The yellow shape hit the Forest floor, sending up clouds of dusty earth.

"Hey! What are you trying to do, break my neck?" The Harp's voice was aggrieved.

Will spluttered and wiped the dirt out of his eyes. He stared in amazement at the thing that had nearly transformed him into one of Luigi's pizzas. It was a huge, maned cat with paws the size of small shields. The creature now lay spread-eagled on the ground, eyeing Rose and Will with an air of disappointed superiority.

Will was petrified. "Is it going to attack?" he whispered.

"It already has," breathed Rose.

"Roar."

"Watch out!" In a single movement, Rose sprang to her feet, grabbed hold of Will's foot and dragged him out of the way.

"R
O
A
R!"

Another of the cat-like creatures plummeted out of the trees, thumping down on the exact spot where Will had been just a split second before.

"Will you knock that off?" howled the Harp.

Rose looked skywards and began to stroll nonchalantly over to the two beasts.

"Are you crazy!" screamed Will. "You'll be killed!"

"Only if they land on me," said Rose. "They're lyons. The laziest hunters in the whole Forest." She ran her hand through the mane of the first lyon.

Will stared, dumbstruck.

"They lie on branches high in the trees, waiting for their victim to stand right underneath them," explained Rose. "Then they roll off their branch, flop down and splat! They fall on their prey and lie on it until it's smothered. Why d'you think they're called ly-ons?" She patted the second lyon. "Then it's dinnertime for all." Both lyons were purring contentedly. "They're deadly in the trees, but as friendly as kittens on the ground. Come and stroke them."

"Or maybe you'd rather keep both your hands?" said the Harp as Will backed away.

"They won't attack you," Rose tried to reassure him. "They'll just lie here until they get bored, then they'll climb back up the tree and lie around, waiting for the next victim."

Will wasn't convinced. He'd seen the sharp teeth that accompanied those purrs. Keeping a wary eye on the two beasts, he picked up his pack and wished for all the world that he was back in Dun Indewood.

If he'd known what was happening in Dun Indewood, Will would have changed his mind. Things were taking a turn for the worse.

Luigi was just putting the finishing touches to a Pasta Blasta when Humfrey burst into the kitchen.

"We have a problem," snarled the boggart. He looked pensive. "Gordin'sh changed his mind."

Luigi let out a laugh. "Tha's a good thing – the one he had before wasn't verra nice!"

"I don't like it." The boggart's nostrils twitched. "I shmell a rat."

"Oh, no! 'Scusi!" Luigi dived towards the oven and wrenched open the door. Spluttering as black smoke poured out, he thrust in a gloved hand and brought out a small, blackened object with four paws and a long tail.

Luigi looked at it sorrowfully and tutted. "The 'ouse special is off."

Humfrey stared at the smoking rodent. "Very appropriate," he drawled. "The Runemashter's gonna be in a shimilar condition very shoon. Gordin'sh bought forward the date of the burning. It'sh tomorrow."

Luigi dropped the burnt offering. Hot Dog took his opportunity and wolfed it up.

"Tomorrow! Rose and Will won' be back by then! What are we gonna do?"

Humfrey winked. "Don't worry, I have a plan…"

Chapter Twenty-One

How Luigi gained a Son and how Will stood in Danger of Being Eaten by a Sandwitch.

Will rubbed his eyes. He'd never seen anything like it before. After several more hours of hard walking, chopping and complaining, he and Rose had seen unexpected tints of gold through the trees ahead of them. Moments later, they were standing at the edge of an oasis of yellow amid the dark gloom of the Forest.

The ground was covered with pale golden sand and pebbles. Strange, six-clawed animals scuttled around the base of the trees. One of them seemed to be weaving a web.

Will stared at it. "What's that?"

"Spider crab," said Rose. She looked around. "Oh dear..."

A few donkeys wandered aimlessly about. Large white birds flew overhead, diving and squawking. Will felt something plop on his shoulder. It was white and didn't smell very nice.

The trees were covered with bright yellow, spade-shaped leaves. Large seed pods, vaguely bucket-shaped and in all the colours of the rainbow, hung from the branches.

"Weird trees," said Will slowly. "What are they?"

"Beach trees," explained Rose.

Will looked worried. "I'm suddenly feeling an irresistible urge to roll up the bottoms of my britches and wear a knotted handkerchief on my head."

The Harp played a jangly little tune and started to sing:

> *"Oh, I do like to be beside the tree side*
> *Oh, I do like to be beside the tree!"*

Will nudged it with his elbow. "What d'you think you're doing?"

"Sorry." The Harp sounded embarrassed. "Don't know what came over me."

Rose bit her lip. "I don't like the look of this. I've heard of this place, but I thought it was just a legend."

"What's the legend?"

"Well, this place was once a seashore."

"What's a seashore?"

The Harp rolled its eyes. "You know, you really should get out more."

"The edge of the sea." Rose held her hand up to forestall Will's next question. "A sea is like a big lake, but I mean *big*. So big you can't see to the other side."

Will whistled. The biggest body of water he had seen was Jenny's pool. "So where's the sea now?" he asked.

Rose shook her head. "Nobody knows. The water retreated and Forest grew across the seabed. But in this place, the plants and animals that had lived on the seashore didn't die out. They're still here."

Will looked around curiously. "Why?"

Rose seemed reluctant to continue. "Well, the legend says," she went on at last, "that this particular part of the seashore was home to a mermaid – that's a kind of water-sprite that lives in the sea – and this mermaid fell in love with a man, a forester. For love of him, she stayed behind when the waters retreated. Around her dwelling, the seashore remained."

"What happened to her?"

"The man betrayed her. He left her for a human woman. The story says she was overcome with grief and rage, and vowed to remain where she was forever, although the sea was no longer there. And she vowed that she would have vengeance upon any man who came within her grasp."

"Oh," said Will.

"Sounds like a really well-adjusted type," said the Harp. But not very loudly.

Rose made an effort to be cheerful. "Of course, it's only a story. Just be careful where you walk. You don't want to be caught by zoomsand."

"Zoomsand?"

"It's like quicksand, only a lot faster." Rose sniffed. "Just the sort of thing you would fall into."

Will glared at Rose. "There you go again!" he snapped. "Why should it be me who falls into it?" He picked up the Harp and stomped off down the track. "Why is it you always think I'm going to be the one that gets into trouble? Why is it...*Whaahhhh*!"

Will's world suddenly collapsed.

He'd found zoomsand.

"Rose! Help!" His screams were silenced as the sand poured into his mouth. His hearing was cut off as his ears filled up with the golden grains.

Will's last sight was of Rose mouthing something. She was reaching out to him...

Then there was nothing but darkness.

The two guards standing at the castle gate were perplexed. Coming up the hill towards them were Hot Dog (pulling the pizza delivery cart), Luigi and... the guards looked at each other and raised their eyebrows... another small, dreadlocked figure.

The multicoloured duo pulled up at the gates.

"'Ow's it goin', boys?" Luigi effused.

The taller of the two guards nodded towards the smaller 'pastafarian'. "Didn't know you had kids, Luigi."

"Ah, s'my li'l secret, boys. This is ma verra own son – Luigi Junior." Luigi tousled his 'son's' dreadlock wig. "'E's no' bad for a such a li'l fella."

The second guard eyed 'Luigi Junior' suspiciously. He could have sworn he heard a mutter of something that sounded like, "Wisheguy".

"So what are yer doing 'ere?" he growled. "We ain't ordered any pizzas."

"Is another surprise!" exclaimed Luigi. "Don' you know what today is?"

"Of course," replied the taller guard matter-of-factly, "It's Widdlesday. And tomorrow's Fursday and yesterday was Phewsday," he added. "So what?"

Luigi gave him a big grin. "Today is a verra special day. I's the Feast of Peasta. All pastafarians celebrate it. And i's our custom to give away free pizza to all our customers." He beckoned towards his 'son'. "Right, Junior?"

There was a whirl of coloured hair as Humfrey nodded agreement with his 'dad'.

"An' then we all give each other Peasta Eggs an' the Peasta Bunny comes an'..." Luigi yelped as 'Luigi Junior' kicked him on the shin. "So I'm givin' you all a free pizza!" he hastily concluded.

The guards' eyes lit up. "Free pizza! For us!"

Luigi held out his hands. "Tha's right! For you and the other guards."

The guard smiled appreciatively. "We can eat it at the burning. It'll be just like a barbecue!" he chortled.

"So the Runemaster's not been burnt yet?" asked Luigi.

"No, he's not one of yer pizzas!" guffawed the smaller guard. "He's still in the Great Hall. We're bringin' him down later."

There were two sighs (and one pant) of relief.

"Shame about the Runemaster," reflected the taller guard. "He was a bit of screwball, but in a likeable sort of way."

"Ay," agreed the other guard. "To think of it. Murdered by Willum the pig kid." He scowled. "I always said he weren't to be trusted. Lettin' a commoner mingle with the Quality, I ask yer. It's like the sayin' says: 'A leopard can't change its underwear'."

"Spots," corrected the taller guard.

"Yeah, I daresay he's got those as well. He was no good from day one."

Luigi wagged a finger. "There's also another sayin': 'Don't judge a pizza by its toppin'. Speakin' of the which..." Luigi handed pizzas to the guards. "'Appy Peasta!" he breezed.

The guards took the offering and opened up the gate. Luigi, Humfrey and Hot Dog moved quickly into the castle, leaving the two guards arguing about who should get the pizza with the olives.

Once inside the courtyard, Humfrey took over proceedings. "Bring the bag and shome pizza. We need an alibi, if we get dishturbed." He pulled his wig down tightly over his head and rolled his sleeves up. "Letsh get down to biznish."

I can't be dead, thought Will as he coughed sand from his dry throat. I'm sure being dead is more comfortable.

He opened gritty eyes and looked around – or tried to. It was pitch dark. Cautiously, he rolled over on to his knees.

"Ow!" The Harp's complaint was muffled. "Get off me, you big ox! I've got sand in my soundbox." The Harp paused to consider. "Hey, where are we?"

"I've no idea." Will began to feel his surroundings with outstretched hands.

They seemed to be in some sort of tunnel, with curved sides of packed earth (or sand, Will thought), which was damp and smelled musty. He must be underground; the tough fibres his fingers brushed against were probably tree roots.

Will reached into his pocket and brought out Rose's tinderbox. He placed a tiny pile of wood fibre in the lid and began to strike at the flint. Eventually, he managed to make a spark and produce a dim glow from the kindling.

"What are you doing?" demanded the Harp as the light of the tiny fire grew. "What do you think you're going to burn?"

Will gave it a hard stare.

The Harp's voice grew shrill with indignation. "Don't even think about it!"

Will grinned lopsidedly. "I'm just trying to see where we are."

"You've got a warped sense of humour, laughing boy," grumbled the Harp, still eyeing Will suspiciously. "I get nervous when people start... *whup!*"

The Harp's voice tailed off in a moan of terror. Will turned slowly.

In the dim light he saw the figure that had crept up the tunnel behind him.

Its upper body was roughly that of a woman, but that was where any resemblance to anything human ended. The creature had a fish tail and dragged itself painfully along the tunnel with its arms, its tail flexing to drive it forward like a snake.

It was made entirely of sand.

"Welcome," it said, in a voice like the hiss of waves on a shingle beach. "I am the Sandwitch and I will be your courier during your... brief... stay here."

The Harp quivered. "This is not good. This is not good at all."

Will felt his heart sink. "Where is here, exactly?"

"At the bottom of my sandpit. If you have any problems," the hissing voice continued, "just come to me, and I will do my best to add to them." The eyeless face was twisted into an expression of pure malevolence. "I have organised a full programme of events for your enjoyment," the Sandwitch continued. "This will begin with swimming and beach volleyball, followed by a delicious meal prepared in the traditional local manner."

Will gawped at the Sandwitch in horror. "Are you serious?"

"No – I lied about the swimming and the volleyball."

Will backed slowly down the tunnel. The Sandwitch dragged herself slowly but relentlessly in pursuit. Then Will remembered the legend. "You're the mermaid," he whispered.

The Sandwitch stopped. Its voice rose in a keen of pain and hatred. "Yes! Once! Once, I welcomed visitors to my pool, to sport and play and forget their cares. I put on beach parties for them... donkey rides... fancy-dress competitions..." The Sandwitch gave a shriek of rage. "But then, that two-timing, double-crossing rat ran out on me. I was just a holiday romance to him." Her body racked with sobs. "He left me here to suffer forever. My pool dried up, I shrivelled in the heat of the sun, but I could not die. Now, I will have my revenge." The creature stretched out her arms towards Will.

"About this meal you mentioned..." Will's voice shook. "That would be me, would it?"

The Sandwitch leered. "My pool is dry. The moisture in your body will make me strong."

"And you said something about the 'traditional local manner'?"

"I shall flay your living flesh until there is nothing left but your bleached and naked bones."

The Sandwitch reared up and opened her mouth impossibly wide. The tunnel was suddenly filled with a storm of whirling sand particles. They tore at Will, striking his skin with terrible force. He opened his mouth to scream and searing grains tore in, scouring his throat, invading his nose and ears, scoring his eyes...

The fragile fireglow from the tinderbox dimmed and went out, leaving Will alone and blind in the roaring, stinging darkness.

Chapter Twenty-two

Of Fiery Gnats and Rampaging Beetles, and how Will looked into the Droppings of a Dragon.

Luigi and Humfrey stood in the Great Hall. Flowers (wilted) and candles (mostly burnt out) surrounded the Runemaster's lifeless body, which lay on a funeral bier in the middle of the chamber. Except for the pastafarian and his 'son' the hall was deserted – all the guards were busy tucking into slices of *Luigi's Thick and Doughy Fat Belly Pizzas* with extra pepperoni. From the guardhouse came sounds of merriment and people swapping onion rings for mushrooms.

Lining the walls of the hall, statues of dead kings stared down in stony silence. All of the Kings of Dun

Indewood had once lain on such funeral beds. Just before they had been burnt.

Humfrey moved purposefully towards the Runemaster. "OK, let'sh take away the empty."

It was easier said than done.

"For such an old man, 'e's a verra 'eavy," panted Luigi as he struggled to pick up the Runemaster.

Humfrey shook his head. "It'sh the weight of responshibility," he explained.

"Well, 'e should lighten up," grunted Luigi as he heaved the body on to his shoulder. "'E's stiffer than a week-old pizza."

Will felt awareness slipping away…

Then, the tunnel was rocked by a series of explosions. The earth shook. The roof cracked. Sand poured down from crevices, rocks and pebbles clattered down, and sunlight poured in.

There was a scream. Will, half-blinded and buried in sand, looked up. Through bleared eyes he saw the Sandwitch raise her hands as a shield against the light…

And he saw the sunlight strike her outstretched arms. The moist sand of which they were made dried in moments and began to trickle. Hands, wrists, forearms and elbows crumbled into dust. Then the full sun struck the Sandwitch's face. She gave a wail of fury and despair as her whole body collapsed in a flow of sandy particles. Within a few moments, all that was left of the terrible, pitiful creature was a little mound of dry sand, sinking into shapeless ruin.

The tunnel roof had completely caved in. Will was now in a sort of deep pit, with light streaming in from above. He blinked more sand from his eyes and looked up. Rose peered over the edge of the pit. She had her fingers in her ears.

"You're all right, then?" she asked brightly, taking them out. "Oh, good."

Will stared at her. "Did you do that?"

"Sorry, you'll have to speak up, I think I've gone a bit deaf."

"There were explosions," Will yelled, in between fits of coughing, "like fireworks. They made the roof fall in and destroyed the Sandwitch. Was that you?"

"Oh, I shouldn't think she's dead," said Rose matter-of-factly. "She'll just sink further into the earth until she finds more moisture and then she'll re-form. I don't think she'll be very pleased when she does."

"What did you do?" demanded Will impatiently.

Rose looked very pleased with herself. "I found some things under the beach trees I thought might help. Of course, I couldn't be sure because I'd only ever heard about them…"

Will took a deep breath. "What – did – you – do?"

"I'm telling you, if you'd only listen. I brought them over here and lobbed them into her sandpit. Bang!" Rose threw her arms wide. "You should have seen it! Great showers of rocks and stones. Anyway, they seem to have done the trick."

Will gaped at her. "Things you found under the beach trees?" he repeated. "What things?"

Rose shrugged her shoulders and said, "Shells."

Humfrey and Luigi were struggling. The dead weight they were carrying was causing the two bodysnatchers to zigzag down the stairs.

"Careful!"

"Hold on!"

"Left!"

"Thish way!"

"Right!"

"Watch your shtep!"

"It's slippin'!"

"Hang on! Don't let go, Luigi!"

Unfortunately, he didn't: and it did.

The figure slipped from four flailing hands and plummeted down the stone stairs, head first.

As one, the two 'removal experts' grimaced.

"Well, that'sh one way of doing it," mused Humfrey. "Letsh get back to your place and hide it."

Luckily, there was no discernible damage. Under the cover of the citadel's doorway, they heaved their burden on to the dogcart and covered it with empty pizza boxes.

Humfrey glared at Luigi. "Hey, what kind'a crummy cart ish thish? It'sh too short! The feet are shtickin' out!"

"It's no' my fault," protested Luigi. "This cart is designed to carry pizza! It's no' a hearse!"

In the end, the two accomplices walked at the back of the cart, one each side, as Hot Dog towed it through the castle gates.

The two guards gave Luigi a cheery thumbs up. "Happy Peasta, Luigi."

"An' to you, boys, an' to you!"

"Does the Feshtival of Peashta exisht?" hissed Humfrey as they passed through the castle gates.

Luigi gave a toothy smile. "It does now! 'Appy Peasta!"

Suddenly, there were no more trees.

The Forest ended at the edge of a plain. Will had grown so used to the relentless march of woodland, the towering trunks around him, the waving branches above and the clinging undergrowth below, that it took him a moment or two to realise that the way ahead lay, not through a forest path, but over a wide plain.

Will raised his head. The change of view wasn't an improvement. The landscape was broken and barren. Boulders lay scattered over crazed slabs of shattered rock. Steam and foul-smelling smoke seethed from fissures. Rising above the plain was the dark and sinister-looking mass of a great mountain. Smoke belched from craters that split its sides like open sores and writhed around its jagged peaks.

Rose stepped up beside Will. "The Ragged Mountain," she said.

Will stared at the dreadful landscape. "Good name."

*Zzzzzzzzzzzzzzzzzzzz*ING!

"Ow!" Will slapped at his neck. "What was that?"

"What was what?"

"Some bug bit me." Will held his hand pressed to the sting.

"That must be one desperate bug," said the Harp and snickered.

Rose eyed Will narrowly. "Let me see."

Reluctantly, Will took his hand away and Rose looked closely at his neck. "It doesn't look like a bite to me. Or a sting. It looks as if you've been…"

*Zzzzzzzzzzzzzzzzzzzz*ING!

"Ow!" Rose clapped a hand to her cheek. When she drew it away, there was a drop of blood on her palm. "Burnt," she said slowly. Her eyes widened. "Uh-oh." She spun around and pointed across the plain. "We've got to get behind those boulders," she said tightly. "Quick!"

Will gaped at her "What? Why?"

*Zzzzzzzzzzzzzzzzzzzz*ING!

"Ow!"

"*That's* why." Rose set off at a run, leaping over boulders and skidding on tilted slabs of stone.

Will bounded after her. "What's attacking us?"

Rose gave him a glance over her shoulder. "Burning gnats."

"Burning gnats?"

Rose crouched, panting, in a gap between two slabs of rock. Will skidded to a halt beside her. "They're insects," Rose told him between gasps. "They live around volcanoes: maybe in them. They get incredibly hot and they fly as fast and as straight as an arrow. They are very, very bad news."

"For you, maybe," sneered the Harp.

"For anything that burns." Rose gave it an evil grin. "That means you too, woodenhead."

"Oh."

Will felt his earlobe gingerly. "Well, they're a nasty pest, but they don't seem too bad..."

"One or two of them don't, maybe. Wait till the swarm finds us."

"What swarm?"

ZzzzzzzzzzzzzzzING!

    ZzzzzzzzzzzzzzzzING!

        ZzzzzzzzzzzzzzzzzzING!

"That swarm."

The air above them was criss-crossed with bright streaks like the trails of shooting stars. Gnats dived down on their shelter, scoring several hits. Without waiting for the look of horror to finish dawning on Will's face, Rose set off again.

Will raced in pursuit, weaving and ducking to try and escape the tiny, burning specks. As he ran, he was dimly aware of a low-pitched drumming, which seemed to come from off to the left. Gradually, the drumming became louder until it was a thunderous roar that filled the air and battered his eardrums.

Will stumbled as the ground began to shake. He saw Rose fall.

He staggered to her over the trembling ground and helped her up.

"What now?" he yelled over the all-enveloping noise. "Is the volcano erupting?"

Rose turned a haggard face to him. "It's worse than that! It's a herd of rhinoceros beetles."

"What are rhinoceros beetles?"

Rose pointed behind him. "Guess!"

Will turned and gave a groan of dismay. Right across the plain, and bearing down on them with terrifying speed, charged a vast army of beetles. They were huge and black, almost as tall as a man, with two wicked-looking horns on their heads. Dust rose behind them in huge clouds.

"Run!" Rose scrambled to her feet and gave Will a shove.

Will ran as hard as ever he could, but it was a hopeless race. Within a few steps, he found himself running between the leading beetles, who turned their giant armoured heads and stared at him incuriously as they skittered past. Just as he felt his lungs would burst, one of the giant insects caught him with a flailing leg. Will crashed head first into a boulder, and saw the advancing black wave rear up to trample him before he passed out.

Several hours later, Will woke up. He was lying in a crack between two rocks. Every inch of his body ached and his head pounded. "Rose?" he called and instantly wished he hadn't.

He staggered to his feet and gazed about with bleary eyes. He was almost at the lower slope of the mountain. The plain was covered in mist and dusk was falling. Will sighed and reached behind him.

There was nothing there.

"Rose," he called again, "can you hear me? I've lost the Harp. Have you got it? Rose?"

There was no reply. Will tried to think. Perhaps the Harp had fallen somewhere close by. He began to search. Further up the slope, he found a patch of mud. Square in the centre of it was a huge, clawed footprint. There was only one creature it could possibly belong to.

"Rose," called Will, "I've found a dragon footprint! Where are you?"

Minutes later, he came across a large pile of ash, steaming gently.

Will stared at it. "Rose," he cried with mounting excitement, "I think I've found a dragon dropping! Can you hear me? Rose?"

The light was fading fast. Will turned and reached out to a strangely shaped rock. It was almost the shape of... yes!

"Rose," he cried, "I've found a dragon's foot!" His gaze travelled up. "And a dragon's leg," he went on slowly. "And a dragon's shoulder. And a dragon's neck." He gulped as a huge, pitiless eye gazed down at him. "And a dragon's head..."

The dragon blinked. Will gulped.

"Oops," he said.

Chapter Twenty-Three

How Rose Beguiled the Dragon and how Humfrey and Luigi were Sent Down for a Long Stretch.

The Dragon of the Ragged Mountain held Will pinned beneath one huge, gnarled claw. Will kicked and struggled to try and pull free. He might as well have tried to push the mountain aside.

The dragon gave him a pained look. *"Stop doing that,"* it complained. *"Prey that wriggles too much tastes nasty."*

"Too bad!" panted Will.

"Exactly!" agreed the dragon. *"Much too bad to eat. When thou strugglest, thy body becomes bitter to the taste. So why dost thou not behave like a sensible prey and keep still while I eat thee?"* It gave Will a long, slow lick in

anticipation. It was like being licked by a cat, but a thousand times worse.

Somewhere in the back of his mind, Will realised that the dragon was speaking to him in human language; but he had no time to wonder about that. He glared at the dragon. "Well, the fact is, I don't want to be eaten. It's bad for my health."

The dragon snorted. *"Thy desires are of no consequence…"*

"You're going about this all the wrong way, you know," a voice interrupted.

Will twitched and looked around in amazement. That was Rose's voice – but where was she?

The dragon's great, golden eyes sparkled in the light of the newly-risen moon as it weaved its head around on its snake-like neck, trying to locate the intruder. *"Where art thou, voice without a body?"*

"Where you can't get at me; otherwise I'd soon be a body without a voice."

The dragon roared. Will covered his ears. The hillside shook; smoke billowed into strange and disturbing shapes; small stones skittered down from the slopes above.

"Temper, temper," said Rose's voice.

"Who art thou?" hissed the dragon.

"A friend."

Will looked up at the dragon and grinned. But not *your* friend, he thought to himself.

The dragon seemed to realise this. It reared up and beat its wings. *"I am the Dragon of the Ragged Mountain,"* it boomed. *"I am Greywing. I do not need friends!"*

"But I want to help you," Rose's voice went on. "You want that boy to stop struggling before he gets too nasty to eat. You've tried persuasion and it hasn't worked. Do you know why?"

"No," said the dragon reluctantly. *"Why?"*

"Because humans never want to do what you ask them to. Particularly boys, for some reason," said Rose's voice pointedly. Will made a mental note to have a word with her about that remark later. If there was a 'later'.

"You'll never get a boy to do anything by asking," Rose's voice continued. "You need to apply reverse psychology."

"Psy-chology?" said the dragon. It sounded uncertain.

"I mean, you want to get inside his head."

"Exactly!" The dragon sounded a lot happier at this prospect. *"Then I can suck his brains out. They are always the tastiest bit."* Will flinched as the dragon licked its chops with a tongue the size of a tablecloth.

"No!" cried Rose hurriedly. "Look, if you can't persuade him to be eaten, why don't you pretend you *don't* want to eat him?"

The dragon looked blank. It made an uncertain little humming noise. It opened its mouth once or twice and shut it again. Eventually, it gave a cough and said hesitantly, *"I am afraid I must be missing thy point. Exactly what is that supposed to accomplish?"*

The voice clicked its tongue. "Don't you realise that forbidden things are always the most desirable?"

"Are they?"

"Of course! When you go raiding, what do you like eating best – humans or cows?"

"I do not go raiding any more," said the dragon sadly. *"Of course, when prey comes to me, that is different."* It gave Will another lick.

"All right, but when you did go raiding, which did you like best?"

"Humans," the dragon answered immediately. *"Especially little girls. They were always tender and juicy…"*

Will grinned. He could imagine Rose's face.

"Yes, yes, yes!" the voice said impatiently. "But the point is, which got you into most trouble – eating little girls or eating cows?"

"Eating little girls, of course; nobody used to miss a few cows, but if I stole little girls they used to send Knyghts on horseback and…" the dragon stopped. *"I think I see what thou meanest,"* it said thoughtfully.

"There you are!" Rose's voice said triumphantly. "If you tell that boy you don't want to eat him, he'll think, 'Hey! What's wrong with me? What have other boys got that I haven't got? Are you calling me stringy or something?'"

"He would not mind me eating him?"

"He'd *beg* you to eat him!"

The dragon opened its eyes wide in wonderment. In a much softer voice, it said, *"That sounds logical. My thanks, Voice."*

"Don't mention it."

The dragon cleared its throat. It looked down at Will. *"Now, listen to me, Prey,"* it said uncertainly. *"I shall not eat thee."*

Will gazed up at it in feigned horror. "Oh!" he cried in a disappointed tone. "You can't mean it!"

"I do mean it," said the dragon with more confidence. *"I would not have thee boiled, baked or fried."*

"That's it!" whispered Rose's voice encouragingly.

"Yes!" The dragon was getting carried away. *"I would not nibble so much as thy little finger if thou wert covered all over with sauce of the barbecue!"*

Acting for all he was worth, Will said brokenly, "Can't I persuade you to change your mind?"

The dragon drew itself up proudly. *"No! That is my final word."*

"I'm deeply disappointed." Will managed to choke out a sob. "But if that's the way you feel, I suppose I may as well be going."

"Oh... ah, very well." The dragon lifted its claw away from Will.

Will took a few steps. He longed to run, but he knew the creature would pounce in a flash once it realised it had been tricked. He forced himself to turn and face the dragon again. "Are you *quite* sure...?"

Sternly, the dragon shook its head. Will let his shoulders droop and set off dejectedly down the hill. It was all he could do to stop himself breaking into a run. Where was Rose?

"Pssst!" A hand was beckoning from a cleft in the rock

to Will's left. He stepped towards it and peered in. It seemed to be the entrance to a cave.

Rose's face scowled at him from the darkness. "I thought you were going to overdo it..." Her voice was drowned by a dreadful roar of rage from higher up the hillside.

Rose turned pale. "I think that dragon has just worked out the flaw in the argument. Come on!" She dragged Will between the rock walls. It was a tight fit and Will only just managed to get inside the cave before the stone around them shook under the impact of several tons of seriously angry dragon.

Back in the City, Humfrey and Luigi were about to enjoy a celebratory meal. Humfrey's mouth watered as Luigi appeared from the kitchen with an enormous steaming bowl of pasta.

"Oh, boy!" Humfrey reached for his fork. "Wadda we got here?"

"Is-a Pasta Pavarotti!" Luigi beamed.

Humfrey eyed the gigantic bowl ravenously. "I may jusht have to climb in there and eat my way out." He raised his fork...

There was a thunderous knocking at the door.

Humfrey looked up with a scowl and Luigi flapped his apron at the door. "Go 'way! We're closed."

"Open in the name of Lord Gordin!"

Luigi and Humfrey exchanged glances. Before they could move, the door burst inwards and a dozen guards poured into the restaurant.

Lord Gordin strode in after them. He placed his clenched fists on his hips and glared at Luigi and Humfrey.

"What have we here?" he growled. "A pastafarian… and a boggart." He leaned forward until his fleshy jowls were quivering inches from Humfrey's face. "Correct me if I'm wrong," he went on dangerously, "but I seem to recall banishing all boggarts and similar lesser races from the City."

"Who are you calling a lesher race, flatfoot?"

"Silence when you speak to the High Lord!" barked the guard commander.

"On the contrary," said Lord Gordin, quelling the unfortunate guard with a look, "silence is the last thing I want. A certain – article – in my possession has gone missing and I am given to understand that a well-known pizza delivery man and…" He glared at Humfrey, "…and his *son* were seen in the vicinity."

"Uh-oh," murmured Humfrey to Luigi, "shomebody musht have sheen us and shpilled the beansh."

Luigi stuck his stomach out proudly. "We don' know nothin'!"

"Very well." Gordin signalled to his men. "Arrest them." Guards came forward with chains and began to shackle Humfrey and Luigi. "You have the right to remain silent," Gordin told them. "In fact, I hope you do. I shall enjoy torturing you until your tormented souls scream for release."

"Our shoulsh schcream for releashe?" Humfrey shook his head. "Shoundsh dishgushting."

Gordin gestured impatiently. "Take them to the dungeons!"

"Dungeonsh!" Humfrey gave a groan as he and Luigi were led away. "I hate dungeonsh!"

Will tugged at a rock with bleeding fingers. "Why didn't you answer when I was calling you?"

"And let the dragon catch me too?" Rose's voice was scornful. "I've warned you before about drawing attention to yourself. Now we're stuck in here *and* you've managed to lose the Harp."

Will was too tired to argue. He stepped back from the rockfall and wiped the sweat from his eyes. "It's no good," he said. "The dragon must have brought half the mountain down behind us. We'll just have to find another way out."

"How do we do that?" Rose said in her most annoyingly reasonable voice. "We can't see a thing."

"Well, we'll have to feel our way through the caves."

"And how do we keep from getting separated?"

"I suppose we'll have to... er... hold hands."

There was a silence. Then Rose said accusingly, "You're loving this, aren't you?"

"No! Look, I don't want to hold hands with you..."

"Oh, thank you very much."

Will kept his mouth shut. One thing he had learnt was that, where Rose was concerned, he was never going to win an argument.

Then he felt a small hand slip into his own. "But only until we're out, all right?" said Rose pugnaciously.

"All right."

Actually, Will had to admit that holding hands with Rose made him feel better about wandering blindly through the caves. In all other respects, the journey was thoroughly disagreeable.

They moved forward at a snail's pace, testing each step. Rough rock grazed their knuckles and Will (who was taller) constantly banged his head. There was no light and no sound except for the steady drip-drip of water from the roof, much of which found its way down their necks. They often had to crouch and sometimes crawl. The floor was uneven and slippery with mud.

It was hot too. The rock groaned and trembled around them. Several times they had to inch past hissing jets of steam, or smoke that caught at their throats, making them cough.

A long, miserable time later, Will stopped suddenly and squeezed Rose's hand.

"Ow!"

"Sssh!" hissed Will. "I think I see light ahead."

The dim glow grew steadily brighter as they crept forward. At last, they found themselves standing in a tunnel mouth that opened on to the floor of a vast cave with softly glowing walls.

Will gazed around in wonder. "It's beautiful! Where does the light come from?"

Rose shrugged. "Fireflies glow in the dark. Some kinds of fungus do too. Must be something like that." She snatched her hand out of Will's with an if-you-ever-tell-anyone-about-this-you're-dead look and stepped forward into the cave.

"Come back," hissed Will. "It could be dangerous!"

Rose glared. "Dangerous compared to what? To being lost in trackless caverns without food or water?" She snorted. "I'll take my chances."

Muttering rude things under his breath, Will followed.

"Hey!"

Rose stared at Will. "Was that you?"

"No. Wasn't it you?"

"No."

"Hey! Over here!"

Will and Rose exchanged glances, then crept towards the sound. In the centre of the cave was a mound that seemed to glitter in the dim light. The voice was coming from the far side of it.

"I know it's you! Come on, move it!"

"I know that voice," said Will slowly.

Rose stopped dead. "Oh, no!" she said bleakly.

The Harp lay halfway up the mound. Its strings were jangling angrily. "You took your time."

"It's really average to see you too," Rose told it. "Let's

save the tearful reunions for later. Do you know the way out of here?"

"Ah – er, yes, I'm glad you mentioned that…" The Harp's voice was low and worried. "There's something you should know…"

Will started to climb the slope. "Hang on, we'll have you down from there in a minute…"

"Yes – look, about this mound…"

Will slipped back. "Hey, this stuff is really hard to climb! It's not solid – what's it made of? It feels like bits of metal…"

"That's what I'm trying to tell you; it's not a mound exactly…"

Rose picked up a handful of the mound and let it fall from her fingers. There was a series of 'ching's. "You're right, this is a very weird mound," she said slowly. "It's made of coins and stuff… gold coins…"

"Yes, well, you see, that's because it's not so much a mound," said the Harp miserably, "as a hoard."

There was a sudden rush of air. Rose and Will looked up in horror as, with lazy strokes of its great, leathery wings, the Dragon of the Ragged Mountain spiralled down from a perch high above and settled on its treasure.

"How very kind of thee to drop in."

Chapter Twenty-Four

How Will and Rose met Tarkwin the Wise and how the Harp Wised Up.

"We meet again, Prey." The dragon turned to Rose. *"The voice, I presume."*

Rose was the first to recover. She glared defiance at the great beast. "Who are you calling prey?" she demanded.

The dragon gave her a surprised look. *"It standeth to reason. Thou art not a dragon and anything that is not a dragon is prey."* The dragon sounded pleased with itself. *"That is logic."*

"Leave us alone!" cried Will. "Or we'll wriggle so much we'll taste awful." He bounced up and down, waving his arms about. "Wriggle, wriggle…" He gestured at Rose, who was staring at him in astonishment. "Come on, wriggle wriggle…"

"Save thy energy," drawled the dragon. *"Since thou hast found my hoard, I shall have to devour thee regardless."* It paused, considering. *"I must say, thou art very persistent. Most treasure-seekers are put off by my guardians…"*

"You mean the gnats? And the beetles?" said Rose. "You've made slaves of them, have you?"

The dragon stamped angrily. *"I merely encourage them to live around my home to discourage intruders. Dragons do not keep slaves. We are creatures of honour."*

"You? A creature of honour?" Will pointed an accusing finger at the great beast. "You are a thief!"

The dragon roared with fury. *"Thou art the thieves! I have stolen nothing!"*

"We're no thieves!" cried Rose. "We've only come here to take back what is ours."

The dragon lowered its great head until its dreadful muzzle was inches from Rose's face. *"What sayest thou?"* it hissed.

"You heard! You came to Dun Indewood and stole the Dragonsbane! We've come to get it back."

The dragon gave her a disdainful stare. *"Thou art mad! I have not been to thy City. I do not have the thing of which thou speakest."*

"He is telling the truth."

Rose and Will spun round in shock at the sound of a new voice. It was cracked and frail, but it was a voice of authority, used to giving commands. A cloaked figure was shambling towards them. Leaning on a staff, it hobbled slowly over the uneven floor. The dragon turned its head to follow the figure's painful progress. The look in its eyes seemed almost to be one of concern.

"Why hast thou left thy bed?" it asked gently.

"Thou hast need of my counsel," the tired old voice said. The speaker turned to Will and Rose. "Greywing has not left his mountain these many years. He has not been to thy City. I swear this to thee."

Will shook his head in bewilderment. Rose took a step towards the stooped figure. "Who are you?" she asked.

The stranger drew back his hood, revealing a wrinkled face older than any they had ever seen. "When I lived among men," he said gravely, "I was called Tarkwin the Wise."

"These manlings are disturbing thee," said the dragon, sounding both concerned and jealous. *"I shall roast them before they overtax thy strength."*

"No!" Feeble as Tarkwin's voice and gesture were, the dragon held back, growling deep in its throat. Tarkwin turned to the travellers. "Come to my chamber. There is much to discuss. I have a story to tell thee."

The dragon followed like a gigantic mother hen while Rose and Will helped the old man back to his cot; then it lay outside the chamber, which was much too small for it to enter, gazing in with one gleaming eye. Time passed. The dragon's breath whistled eerily through the dank, dimly lit cavern as Tarkwin told his story.

When he had finished, Will paced angrily up and down the old man's cell. His shadow, distorted and enlarged by the light of a blazing fire, swept across the bare stone walls, back and forth, back and forth.

He stopped and turned to face Tarkwin. "So you stole the Dragonsbane the first time!"

The old man gave a sad half-smile and nodded.

"Then the Runemaster came and took the stone back. So you came to Dun Indewood and snatched the stone while his mind was inside it so he couldn't tell anyone that you were the thief!"

This time, Tarkwin shook his head. His voice was noticeably weaker. "I suspect that what the Runemaster told thee was not the truth…"

"Are you saying the Runemaster was lying?" demanded Will hotly. The dragon hissed a warning.

Tarkwin waved a feeble hand. "No, no. I do not say he lied. Yet there is much he does not understand." The old man closed his eyes and beckoned Will and Rose closer. "Listen…

"I brought the Dragonsbane away from Dun Indewood, that is true; but not to learn its secrets or add its power to mine. I took it because I had reason to believe that the new High Lord could not be trusted."

"Gordin," breathed Will.

"The new High Lord's family had a wicked reputation. For years, there had been rumours that they were linked with renegade sorcerers and dark magic. The night Gordin was elected, I cast the runes. They showed me that Gordin

Mandrake planned to use the Dragonsbane to enslave the people of Dun Indewood. I had no time to make plans or even to inform my apprentice…"

"The Runemaster," said Rose.

"There was no time to tell him what I planned to do. I took the stone from the Treasury, and left the City for the Dark Forest. I could not entrust the stone to a human Lord, because he might misuse it, as Gordin had planned to do. And the dragons would not take it. If one dragon had offered to keep the Dragonsbane, he would have been cast out by the others."

"No dragon would enslave another," hissed Greywing from the doorway. *"No dragon would allow itself to be enslaved."*

"Eventually," Tarkwin continued, "I came to the Ragged Mountain and fell in with Greywing. Here was my solution. Greywing, a dragon, was stronger than I. I, with the Dragonsbane, was more powerful than he: we could destroy each other. So we agreed a truce. Greywing was already an outcast. He had nothing to lose by harbouring the stone. With his protection, I had nothing to gain by using it. So I came to live here."

The old man fell silent for so long that Will thought he had gone to sleep. "Then the Runemaster came…" he prompted.

Tarkwin opened his eyes. His voice was growing fainter. "Yes. He found out where the Dragonsbane was. He lured Greywing away and came here in search of it. He accused me of treachery: of being in league with a dragon, which was partly true, and of stealing the stone for my own purposes, which was wholly false. I tried to explain, but he was too angry to listen. He attacked me. I had performed no magic for many years. I could not withstand him. He overcame me. By the time I came to my senses, he had gone and the Dragonsbane with him."

"Thou wouldst not let me pursue him," muttered Greywing discontentedly.

"I could not send a dragon against a human," Tarkwin told him, "and he was a wizard; a powerful adversary even for thee, brother." The dragon huffed.

"As you see, I had not the strength to follow him myself," the old man continued in a voice that was growing more feeble with every passing moment. "Indeed, I have very little time left."

"But it was a dragon that took the stone," Will insisted. "Humfrey inquestigated the Runemaster's room and he was sure of it. And Luigi's customer saw a dragon. If the thief isn't Greywing, it must be another dragon."

"No." The dragon's voice was decisive. *"If any other dragon held the stone, I would know of it."*

"This is crazy." The Harp's voice was sharp with exasperation. "The old guy is too sick to have done it, and he says the dragon didn't do it, and the dragon says none of the other dragons did it. So for crying out loud, who *did* do it?"

Rose knelt beside Tarkwin and took the old man's hand. "Did the runes tell you what Gordin planned to do with the stone?"

Tarkwin's voice was little more than a whisper as he said, "They did not. The runes are often unclear. Perhaps I had too little understanding."

Will crouched beside the old man's bed. "Can you tell us nothing more?"

"I am almost spent." Tarkwin smiled gently. "Yet I will do what I can." He raised his voice. "Greywing!"

"I hear thee," rumbled the dragon.

"I pray thee, take these two humans to Dun Indewood. The City will have need of them – and so wilt thou and thy kind."

The dragon looked far from happy, but it said, *"I will."* Tarkwin turned to Will. "Bring me the Harp."

"Hey! Don't I get a say in this?" the Harp demanded as Will passed it over. "What if this guy's some sort of harp-hater? What if he wants to play *Chopsticks* on me over and over again? What if… hey! Cut that out!"

The old man held the Harp against his chest. It fell silent and quivered. For a moment, nothing happened. Then a voiceless whispering sound echoed around the cavern as a glowing, silver mist formed in the air surrounding the wizard's wasted form.

Tarkwin stroked the Harp gently. Just on the edge of hearing, he whispered the words of a spell. The silver aura gradually changed to gold and flowed down the old wizard's arms into the Harp. There sounded one crystal-pure, brilliant note, which was at the same time a single note of music and all notes.

Then the mist vanished.

The Harp opened its eyes wide. Its bad-tempered face was transformed by a look of astonishment. "Hey – my memory – he gave me my memory back. Better than ever! The Runemaster – I know who it was who broke in and stole the Dragonsbane." It turned to Will. "You were right all along! Big guy, stumpy legs, face with more holes than a crumpet, little beady eyes: it was Gordin!"

Rose shook her head. "I don't understand," she said. "Humfrey said the thief was a dragon."

Will was silent.

"All right, all right," snapped Rose. "I know you said it was Gordin all along. Maybe we should have listened to you."

Will raised an eyebrow.

"All right, we should *definitely* have listened to you. So what do we do now?"

"There's nothing more we can learn here," said Will. "We have to go back to the City."

"Will..." Rose was staring wide-eyed at Tarkwin.

As Will watched, the old man's hands slipped from the Harp and his head fell back. Tarkwin the Wise was dead. The Dragon of the Ragged Mountain lifted its head from the stone floor. Its wail of sorrow echoed through the underground chambers of its mountain.

CHAPTER TWENTY-FIVE

How Flying caused the Harp to Flap and how Rose and Will took the Underground.

"I want to go down!" screeched the Harp. "Put me down *right now*!"

Rose hauled the howling instrument out of the bag on Will's shoulders and held it out to the side with one hand. "Anything you say."

The Harp looked down – a long way down – and shuddered. "I was thinking maybe we could land first?" it said in subdued tones.

Will gave it an encouraging smile. "We're perfectly safe."

"Safe?!" The Harp's strings hummed violently in the

streaming air and its voice wobbled in a terrified vibrato. "We're flying at very high speed on the back of a dragon, thousands of feet above the ground! You call that safe?"

Will grinned at it. "Enjoy the ride and stop harping on."

"You are not funny..."

Unlike the Harp, Will felt exhilarated. His initial fear of climbing on to Greywing's back had quickly been replaced by the sheer thrill of riding on a dragon.

With a lazy beating of its enormous wings, the Dragon of the Ragged Mountain had soared up into the moonlit sky and headed towards Dun Indewood.

Will smiled at Rose. She was peering at the great swathe of forest below them. In the blue-silver moonlight, the trees were swaying in the wind so that the Forest looked like a vast, ruffled lake. There was no sound but the rush of wind and the whump-whump of the dragon's gigantic wings.

The dragon ride Will had taken in Brightscale's mind when he'd entered the Dragonsbane was nothing compared to the real thing. His senses were heightened, his heart was thumping and he could feel the adrenaline surging through his body. Despite the buffeting wind and numbing cold, Will was ecstatic. This is what Quests were about!

"Look!" Rose pointed. Far off to the North, a dull red glow had appeared below the horizon. "What's that?"

Will stared. "It could be another city like Dun Indewood," he said slowly. "The history books in the

Knyght School library say that once, there were many cities in the Forest. Maybe there still are."

"Or it could be a volcano," Rose pointed out. "Do you know what it is, Greywing?"

"No," said the dragon. *"I have never been so far."*

Will stared into the darkness. What was out there? Lost castles? Ruined towers? Dark cities, full of treasure and danger? One day, he thought, he would find out.

Clearings began to appear below: single dwellings, where the smoke from wood and turf fires made them cough as they flew through it; and small villages, where their appearance was greeted by animal and human cries of alarm, and once by a flurry of arrows that Greywing side-slipped disdainfully to avoid.

"Wahh!" The Harp was not impressed. "You're going too fast! Don't dive like that! Watch the treetops! Be careful of oncoming dragons. Don't... aargggghhhh! You nearly hit that mountain!"

"Silence!" ordered Greywing. *"I hate back-seat drivers,"* the dragon muttered to itself and plummeted into a downwards spiral to prove a point.

Soon (too soon for Will and not soon enough for the Harp), it was over. Greywing lost height in a long glide before dropping neatly into a clearing near Rose's cottage. Rose and Will scrambled off the dragon's back and walked forward, a little unsteadily, then turned and bowed before Greywing.

"Thank you for your kindness," said Will. The dragon dipped its great head, returning the bow.

Will hesitated. "I wasn't sure you would keep your word," he said at last.

The dragon tilted its head in inquiry.

"You had our lives in your power. Anytime you so wished, you could have ended them."

"I promised Tarkwin," answered the dragon solemnly. *"I am a creature of honour. Trust is a sacred thing."*

"Oh, absolutely," sneered the Harp. "And you really are trustworthy. Like you never betrayed the trust of all the other dragons by stealing their gold?"

The Dragon of the Ragged Mountain reared up menacingly. Will gulped and Rose clasped her hand over the Harp's mouth. But the dragon merely drew a deep breath and nodded slowly. Sadness passed across its face and one great tear welled in the corner of its eye.

"Thou speakest true, Harp. But that was in my youth. With age comes wisdom. I have aged and I have learnt. Too late, alas. I have never been a man. I am no longer a dragon."

The dragon opened its great wings. *"And now thou must fulfil thy destiny,"* it said.

"Wait!" Will held up a hand. "Won't you stay here? We may need your help when we get into the City."

"That was not part of my promise to Tarkwin." The dragon shook its great head. *"Suppose the Harp speaks true and thy High Lord hath the Dragonsbane? I would be far away when he discovers its powers."*

Will kept his voice even. "If Gordin learns to control the stone and summon dragons, perhaps nowhere will be too far away."

The dragon shook its head again. *"Even so."* With powerful beats of its wings, it soared upwards. *"Goodbye, manlings!"*

Will watched it out of sight and sighed.

Rose broke the silence. "Come on, let's get back to Dun Indewood. We need to find Humfrey and tell him what's happened."

Will gave a groan of resignation. "I suppose so. Where's your granny's dress?"

Rose grinned. "Why – do you enjoy wearing it?"

"No, I do not!" snapped Will. "But I need it to get into Dun Indewood, don't I? Gordin's guards will still be looking for me."

"Aha!" smiled Rose enigmatically, "Follow me."

"Here we are," said Rose.

Will looked around. "Here we are, where?" he asked. He was confused. After picking up a basket from her cottage, instead of heading towards the West Gate, Rose had led Will into the Forest away from the City. The first light of dawn was breaking as she'd stopped at the foot of a gnarled old tree.

Rose knelt beneath its branches and began clearing leaves and moss from the ground. Will watched her with astonishment, then asked, "What sort of tree is this?"

Rose gave him a big grin. "It's an en-tree."

She heaved at the iron ring she'd uncovered. A trapdoor creaked open, revealing a large hole in the ground with stone steps leading down into pitch darkness. "Trademan's entrance." Rose pointed downwards. "This is how we get into Dun Indewood."

Producing a rushlight from her basket, she led the way underground. Will tried to keep as close to Rose and the light as possible, though it gave little more than a flickering glow in the darkness of the stone tunnel.

"Careful, the ceiling is..."

"Ow!"

"...low and hard."

"Thanks a bundle," moaned Will as he rubbed his head.

Rose laughed. "Luckily it was just your head."

"What do you mean by that?"

The Harp broke into a giggle. "She means you're stupid, stupid."

Will banged the Harp into the wall.

"Oof! Somebody's had a sense of humour bypass."

As they made their way along the roughly-hewn tunnel, Rose told Will its history.

"They say old King Madimus built it," she said, "while he was convinced he was a rabbit."

"A rabbit?"

"Yeah." The Harp snickered. "The old goofball thought he was a big pink bunny called Carroty Ken. He used to come down this tunnel into the Forest to hop about and eat grass."

Will shook his head. "I don't think that's in any of the history books."

"Of course not," said Rose. "They always leave out the best bits."

She went on to explain that later on, Madimus had decided he was really a bird, so he'd stopped using the tunnel. After the last King disappeared it had gradually been forgotten. "It leads into the very heart of the castle," explained Rose. "Very few people know about it."

"So how do you know about it?" asked Will.

"She knows everything," needled the Harp.

Will frowned. "What about Gordin?"

"No," replied Rose. There was a pause, then: "At least, I don't think so," she added uneasily.

"So why didn't we use this way into the City before?" asked Will. "Why did I have to wear a dress?"

"I didn't want to give away all my secrets," Rose replied. "Besides, you looked cute!"

After some time, the passage began to incline upwards.

"We're under the castle," said Rose. "Not far now."

"Why the castle?" demanded Will.

"Because that's where the tunnel comes out," said Rose reasonably. "Then we sneak out of the castle and find Humfrey. Don't worry, it's easy, I've done it loads of times."

Will sighed. Talk about going from the frying pan into the fire, he thought. Then he shrugged. Whatever Rose had planned, he could trust her. He sometimes wondered which, of the two of them, was the real Knyght.

Rose paused at the foot of a wooden ladder. "Up here,"

she whispered. "It leads into the cellars. Follow me and be careful."

The Harp burst into song:

> "Hey dilly-dilly, hey dilly dilly,
> Come and be killed..."

"Shut up," Rose told it.

At the top of the ladder was another trapdoor. Rose lifted it and peered out cautiously. Satisfied, she climbed through the trapdoor. Will followed her into a bare, stone room. He could just see, in the guttering flare of the rushlight, that the room was roughly square with a low ceiling and no door.

"Nice place," drawled the Harp. "Maybe you could fix it up a little – nothing fancy, just a few rats gnawing at skeletons, the odd skull..."

Rose gave the Harp a disgusted look, then crossed the floor and pushed a stone that looked like all the others. A section of wall slid inwards with a faint grinding noise. Signalling for silence, Rose led Will through the secret doorway and into a stone-flagged corridor.

Further up the passage was a large oak door. A sign hung from a nail.

DUNGEON
THE TORTURER IS IN

A sound of approaching footsteps echoed down the

corridor. "Hide," snapped Rose, quickly snuffing out the light and pushing Will into a small recess in the wall. He winced with pain as the Harp, pushed up against the hard stone wall, dug into his ribs.

"Oof! Watch the woodwork, dummy!"

As the footsteps grew louder, Will risked a peep down the corridor – then snapped his head back so fast he banged it on the wall behind him.

The approaching figure was Gordin.

The High Lord stopped outside the dungeon door and flung it open. "Scumbucket!" he roared.

Will raised his eyebrows at Rose. "He's not very polite, is he?"

"That's the torturer's name," whispered Rose. "Roofus Scumbucket."

"Oh."

Gordin's voice rang down the corridor. "Have you found out where these two criminals have hidden the Runemaster's body?"

Will and Rose stared at each other with open-mouthed horror. Gesturing to Will to keep silent, Rose crept along the corridor. Will followed.

Peering through the open dungeon door, they could make out the figure of a man standing next to Gordin. He was dressed in black leather. And on the far wall... Will's heart missed a beat... on the far wall, hanging in chains, were Humfrey and Luigi.

Chapter Twenty-Six

How Humfrey and Luigi hung around and how Lord Gordin took a Turn for the Worse.

Will turned an appalled face to Rose. "What are they doing there?" he hissed.

Rose shook her head. "Something's gone horribly wrong."

Gordin's voice grated menacingly from the dungeon. "Haven't you started the brutal torture yet?"

The torturer nervously shook his masked head. "We're having problems with the equipment, Guv'nor. The thumbscrews won't screw, the branding irons have all melted. You've got us torturin' so many victims, all this gear's on its last legs."

"Even the rack?" Gordin waved at Humfrey. "To help

our small friend become a more normal size," he added maliciously.

The torturer shook his head. "Sorry, Guv'nor, can't get the parts."

Gordin clenched his ham-like fists. "The iron maiden?"

"It's her day off."

Gordin's eyes glittered dangerously. "I meant the fiendish torture machine, you dolt."

"Oh, right. Er, no. The hinges are rusted and the spikes are all blunt."

"Sheer incompetence!" growled Gordin. "Isn't there anything you can do?"

There was a pause as the torturer scratched his head. "Er, I could try tickling 'em," he suggested.

"Tickling them!"

"Yeah, Guv'nor. It always works with my nipper. If I fink he's been bad, I just tickle his feet until he tells me the truth."

The High Lord controlled himself with an effort. "I shall be in the citadel for two hours," he said. "That is how long you have to get the information I want. Otherwise you will lose your job... and several parts of your body," he added menacingly.

Rose and Will dived back into the safety of the recess as Gordin stormed out of the dungeon and stomped angrily away.

"What are we going to do?" hissed Will.

"Rescue them," replied Rose.

"How?"

Rose pointed at her basket and winked. "You stay here."

She walked into the dungeon. Before Luigi and Humfrey could cry out, she put a warning finger to her lips.

"Hello, Mr Scumbucket," she said in her best, sweet, sing-song voice.

The black-clad figure turned round. "What are you doing here?" he growled menacingly.

"The High Lord thought he was a bit rude to you and so he's sent me down to say sorry and no hard feelings."

The torturer looked askance at Rose. "The High Lord says sorry?"

Rose nodded sweetly. "And to make it up, he's sent you some goodies."

"Goodies?"

"In the basket."

"What sort of goodies?"

Rose reached under the blue check cloth that covered the top of the basket. "There's some cakes, some lemonade…"

"Ooh, yummy!"

WHACK! THUMP!

"…and a big stick with a nobbly end," added Rose as she stood over the unconscious body. "Works every time."

"'Oly cannelloni! Way to go, Rose!" yelled Luigi.

"Nicshe move, shishter," drawled Humfrey. "Couldn't have done it better myshelf."

Will found the keys to the fetters on the unconscious

man's belt and set about freeing his friends.

Luigi lowered his arms. "I been hangin' there so long, I feel like a string of spaghetti," he said sorrowfully.

Humfrey rubbed his aching wrists. "What took ya sho long?" the boggart complained.

"It's a long story," Will began.

"Then shave it. We got the Runemashter on ishe…"

"Ishe?"

"Ice," translated Rose.

"That'sh what I shaid, ishe. Did you get the Dragonshbane?"

"No. Gordon has it," said Will. "He stole it from the Runemaster in the first place."

"But that doesn't make shensh. All the evidencsh pointed to a dragon, not Gordin," insisted the boggart.

Will shook his head. "The Harp got its memory back and it says so."

Humfrey looked sceptical. "I wouldn't trusht that cockamamie ukelele ash far ash I could shpit."

The Harp bridled. "Now listen, small stuff…"

Humfrey ignored it.

"You can argue later, *boys*. Right now, we've got to get to the citadel and find out what Gordin's up to." Rose handed Humfrey a crossbow, which he dropped with a clatter.

"Shorry, sishter," he said sheepishly. "My hands aren't workin' worth a darn – I couldn't aim a bow to shave my life."

Rose nodded. "All right, take the Harp."

She pointed at the torturer's sword which Will picked up.

Luigi gave Rose a worried look. "Wha' d'you want me to do?"

Rose smiled. "Oh, don't worry, I've got a special job for you."

A curious group made its way through the castle and out towards the citadel.

"You're supposed to be escorting us," Rose hissed at the black-clad figure behind her. "Try not to waddle."

Luigi wriggled uncomfortably in the torturer's leather clothes. "Is' all ri' for you," he complained. "These trousers are t'ree sizes too small – they're bindin' me right in the pomodoroes."

The few guards they met showed no interest in another group of prisoners being escorted from the dungeons. Once inside the citadel, there were no more guards and Luigi was able to take off the torturer's hood, which had hidden his multicoloured dreadlocks.

The companions made their way up the stone stairs. Raised voices sounded from the upper chamber that had formerly been the Runemaster's bedroom. Humfrey peered cautiously in.

The windowless room was full of smoke and shadows. Gordin was standing in the middle of a circle of candles with Symon at his side. Both were dressed in livid green robes, which shimmered in the candlelight.

Gordin had his back to the stairs. He was holding up the Dragonsbane by its chain, while Symon looked on hungrily.

"By the powers of the Dragonsbane, I command thee, Runemaster, to begone!" boomed Gordin.

There was a pause. Nothing happened.

Humfrey beckoned the others forward. "Now I get it," he hissed. "But Gordin'sh tryin' to use the Dragonshbane. Sheemsh he can't do that while the Runemashter'sh life force ish in there, but he'sh doin' hish darndesht to get him out. Then he'll bump off the Runemashter and Gordin will control the Dragonshbane."

In the circle, Symon shook his head. "It's not working, Dad."

"I know that, fool!" Gordin raised one hand to strike Symon, who cowered. The High Lord regained command of himself with an effort. "Have patience," he grated. "The Runemaster's spirit will be released when his body is destroyed. Then, the powers of the stone shall be ours."

Symon's eyes shone with greed. "How will you find the body, Dad?"

Gordin gave a humourless smile. "I think... I think I should ask his friends." In one flowing movement, the High Lord spun round, sword in hand. "Welcome, Willum – all of you. Do join us. I insist."

Humfrey bit his lip and nodded at the others. They shuffled up the last few stairs and into the chamber, Rose with her crossbow at the ready and Will fingering his sword.

Symon scooted round behind his father. "Do something, Dad."

The High Lord gave his son a contemptuous glare. "Silence, blockhead!" He turned back to face his adversaries. "What an interesting collection," he murmured. "A boggart, a cook, a pig boy and..." he stared hard at Rose, "... a girl."

"And a Harp, don't forget the Harp," rang out a voice from behind Humfrey.

"Oh, I won't, I really won't," said Gordin. "I thought I'd dealt with you already but as you're here, you can help me out with my problem."

"You ain't goin' to get anything out of ush," Humfrey's voice was firm.

"Oh, I think I will. I shall strip all the information I need from your cringing minds and then I'll have you executed."

Will took a step forward. "On what charge?"

"Treason and murder."

"That's two charges," the Harp pointed out.

"Then I'll execute you twice!" Gordin's voice had an uneasy edge to it.

"But it was you who stole the Dragonsbane. And I didn't murder the Runemaster; he's not dead."

Gordin's breathing was becoming heavier.

"Unfortunately, that is true. But not for much longer. Once you tell me where he is, I will remedy that situation. And then..."

Gordin held up the Dragonsbane and Will saw that it was glowing, pulsing as though it was alive. Its light filled the room. Luigi exchanged uneasy glances with Rose and Humfrey.

The High Lord glared at his enemies with such ferocious savagery that they recoiled. "I should have killed you all when I had the opportunity," he snarled.

"Yeah? You and whose army?" The Harp's voice echoed mockingly through the small chamber. "You talk big, but you're just a low-life, two-bit crook, a windbag. Am I right or am I right, ugly?"

Rose made frantic *shush*ing motions at it.

Veins throbbed in Gordin's temples. The High Lord's hands were so tightly clenched that the knuckles showed white. The Dragonsbane bit deeply into Gordin's palm and blood oozed out. The stone glowed even more fiercely.

"You are making me angry, Harp." The High Lord was trembling with fury. "You wouldn't like me when I'm angry."

"I'm not exactly your number one fan when you're happy, knucklehead!" sneered the Harp. "You're just a pipsqueak who thinks he's a heavyweight. Well, let me tell you something..."

Gordin sneezed. A small flame shot from the High Lord's nose and he began to shake violently.

Symon began to back away. "Er... Dad? Are you all right?"

Will's throat grew tight with terror. As he watched in astonishment, the High Lord's eyes began to glow. Their colour changed to gold. The pupils became vertical slits, lizard-like and merciless.

"You will not mock me." Gordin's voice had become a deadly, hissing growl. "I am the High Lord. I am the Mandrake!"

The air fizzed and hummed. Lines of magical force crackled around the High Lord's body as it began to swell and change shape. The candles flared like fireworks, sending jets of flame high into the air, and streams of orange and yellow sparks across the room. Then a rumbling, roaring sound filled the room. Will could feel heat. He could taste it. The air steamed. The room was filled with the smell of the forge, of the furnace, of volcanoes.

"Cover your eyesh!" Humfrey shouted.

The roar grew into an all-consuming crescendo. The citadel shook to its foundations, sending everyone crashing to the floor. Still the noise grew.

There was a final, eye-searing flash and a titanic clap of thunder: then silence. Hesitantly, Will, Rose, Humfrey and Luigi uncovered their ears, opened their eyes and looked up.

The Dragonsbane lay on the stone floor, its fierce glow fading. There was no sign of the High Lord. Where he had been, a dragon stood swaying, its hooked steel claws flexing. Its terrible, pitiless eyes were fixed on Will.

Symon was staring at the creature, paralysed with fear.

"D-d-d-dad?" he quavered.

CHAPTER TWENTY-SEVEN

Of the dangers of Playing With Fire
and how Rose pulls a Fast One.

"Go get 'em, Dad!" Symon's voice was a strange mixture of triumph and terror as he backed into a corner.

Will and his companions stared at the dragon that had been High Lord Gordin.

"Shay," murmured Humfrey, "that'sh kinda impresshive."

"What's happening?" screeched the Harp in shrill complaint from his bag on Humfrey's back. "Turn round! Turn round! I want to see!"

Humfrey obligingly turned round. The Harp gave a strangled twang.

"Turn back! Turn back! I don't want to see!"

The monstrous creature towered above Will, who stood rooted to the spot, too stunned to move. The Gordin-dragon's neck was bowed towards him. Even with its wings furled, its shoulders scraped the ceiling and there was hardly room in the chamber for it to turn its massive body. Its eyes glittered with malice. Will watched in horrified fascination as the great beast that had been High Lord of the City inflated its chest in readiness to emit a blast of fire that would vaporise him where he stood.

"Are you going to stand there all day?"

Rose's shriek broke Will's trance. He threw himself to the right and rolled, just as the dragon belched out a great gout of flame that turned the stone flags where Will had been standing into a puddle of molten rock.

Will sprang up and launched himself at the dragon's head. With all the force he could muster, he brought his sword down on the creature's snout. He might as well have tried to chop an anvil in half. The dragon didn't even blink. Will ducked: another blast of flame seared over his head as he dived beneath the dragon's chin and hacked at its throat. The sword slid off the smooth, hard scales without leaving a mark.

"Here, boy! Fetch!"

The dragon's head swivelled. Rose had taken advantage of Will's attack to grab the Dragonsbane. Now she held it aloft by its chain, waving it as if it was a stick and the dragon a dog.

The furious creature roared and let fly with another burst of flame, but Rose had skipped behind a pillar, which was turned to smoking rubble by the blast.

"Here, boy!" she cried again and threw the Dragonsbane to Humfrey.

"Hot potato," squeaked the Harp faintly. "Pass it on. Quick!"

The boggart flipped the stone to Luigi, who gave a high-pitched squeal of dismay, and juggled it from hand to hand as if it was red-hot. As the dragon swung its head towards him, the pastafarian panicked, lobbed the stone at Will, then closed his eyes and clapped his hands over his ears.

Will dropped the sword and dived for the stone. It bounced off the tips of his fingers. Rose gave a howl of dismay.

Scrambling to his feet, Will kicked the stone from under the dragon's advancing muzzle. He chased the Dragonsbane as it rolled across the floor, scooped it up one-handed, and looked around for Rose. She was waiting by the doorway, through which Humfrey and Luigi were just disappearing.

"To me!" she yelled. Will threw the Dragonsbane to her, then dived to avoid another blast of dragon-fire. Rose caught the stone neatly and vanished through the archway, which an instant later exploded in a crackling roar of flame.

Bellowing with fury, the Gordin-dragon hunched its great shoulders. There was a groaning creak of tortured wooden beams and then the ceiling splintered and part of the wall fell away. The dragon scrambled up and out of the wreckage, spread its great wings and beat into the air above the citadel. Panic-stricken shrieks echoed from the castle as the gigantic beast appeared above the rooftops.

As he gazed at its retreating form, Will sensed a movement behind him. Instinctively, he ducked as a sword whistled over his head, then spun round to face Symon.

"Now I've got you, pig boy!" The Lordling's eyes were wild and staring. He was holding the sword Will had dropped. "You've been in the way for long enough," he howled and swung again.

Symon was no fighter, but he had a sword and Will didn't. What's more, Symon was attacking in a sort of panic-stricken fury. Will dodged and leapt across the rubble of the ruined chamber, trying to keep out of the way of the lethal sweeps.

Then Symon stumbled. His sword sliced across Will's chest, slashing his tunic and nicking the skin beneath; but then it flew wide as Symon flung out his hands to save himself. Seizing his opportunity, Will leapt forward and barrelled into Symon, knocking him to the ground.

The fight instantly went out of Symon. Will knelt astride him, fists clenched, but Symon lay limp and burst into tears.

"Again," he cried in a choking voice, "again! You're always better. I'm the High Lord's son and you're a pig boy, but you were always better – than – me..." Symon choked back his sobs and his eyes narrowed spitefully. "But my dad'll get you. He'll get you if you touch me. He will, he will!"

Will stared down at Symon. The High Lord's son was a pitiful spectacle, his face blubbered with tears and stained with blood. Will remembered what he had read in Symon's books. A Good Knyght should show mercy to his fallen enemy and treat him with kindness.

That's what a Good Knyght should do. That's what the book said.

Will drew back his fist and gave Symon a punch to the jaw that made his teeth rattle and knocked him out cold. He *would* be a Good Knyght one day – but not today.

"Ow!" Will blew on his throbbing knuckles and sucked them. Then he grabbed the sword and went to find Gordin.

Will raced into the castle courtyard. Two of Lord Gordin's guards had dropped their spears and were trying to hide behind each other. Will followed their terrified gaze. Above him, the Gordin-dragon hovered over the castle towers. It was burning roofs and smashing windows, totally ignoring the occasional guard who was brave or foolish enough to try shooting at it with a crossbow.

Will had no clear plan in mind. He only knew that Gordin must be stopped. He raced unceremoniously through the Ceremonial Doorway, barged his way through crowds of panic-stricken Knyghts and Counsellors, who were rushing around giving contradictory orders and looking for good places to hide, and took the Grand

Staircase three steps at a time. At the top, he ran full pelt into Gyles, who sat down abruptly with an "Oof!"

"Gyles!" Will helped his friend up. "Have you seen Rose?"

Gyles gazed at him wide-eyed. "Will! What's happening? Doctor Blud was looking out of the window just now – then he screamed, told us to take the rest of the day off, and went and locked himself in the privy. Everybody's leaving the castle. What's going on?"

"I'll tell you later!" yelled Will. "Where's Rose?"

Gyles shrugged. "A girl came through here a minute or two ago. She was heading for the main tower. Will, what's…?"

But Will had already gone, racing up the winding stairways of the castle, his legs growing heavier with every step. Gasping, he burst through the turret door on to the battlements of the main tower.

Rose stood between him and the battlements with her hands clasped behind her back. Hovering in front of her, its reptilian mouth set in a snarl and its eyes glittering with rage, was the dragon.

"I expect you want your stone back, don't you?" she was saying in a soothing voice.

The dragon raised its head and gave a roar of fury that shook tiles from roofs all over the City.

"Yes, I thought so – but I haven't got it, you see." Rose held out her left hand and opened it. "Nothing in this one." She put her left hand behind her back and pulled out her right. "And nothing in this one."

Gordin roared again.

"No, I haven't been swapping hands. I gave the Dragonsbane to Humfrey and Luigi so they could revive the Runemaster." Rose held both hands out for the dragon's inspection. They were empty.

Rose turned; she cannoned into Will. The impact drove him through the door and sent them both tumbling down the narrow stairway, while the dragon's flaming breath scorched the battlements above them and its wingbeats sent stones toppling from the tower.

Rose landed on top of Will, who pushed her away and glared at her. "Why did you tell him that? Now the dragon will be after Luigi and Humfrey!"

Rose shook her head. "No, Will, that's what…"

"Stay here!" Will set off down the tower. "I'm going to find them!"

"Will, wait! It's not what…"

But Will had gone. Rose snorted in disgust. "Boys! Why don't they ever *listen*?"

In the cellar of *Luigi's Fasta Pasta on the Piazza*, Humfrey flung open the wooden lid of Luigi's enormous flour bin. He and the pastafarian thrust their arms up to their shoulders inside. Straining and heaving, they hauled a stiff and motionless figure from its concealing bed of flour. For a moment they stood coughing, surrounded by billowing clouds of white powder. Then they began the hard task of dragging the extraordinarily heavy, flour-coated figure up the cellar steps.

Still coughing, sneezing and blinking flour from their eyes, they stumbled out of the restaurant door into the piazza. Here, they set their burden down for a moment while Humfrey made a feeble attempt to dust himself off and Luigi wiped flour from his face with his apron. As they bent to lift their load once more, a menacing rumble sounded from directly above them.

The Harp, still hanging from the boggart's back, quivered. "Don't look now, boys," it said faintly, "but we've got company…"

Humfrey and Luigi looked up.

They began to back away: very, very slowly.

Moments later, Will raced into the square. He gave a cry of horror. Luigi and Humfrey were running for their lives, but the dragon was hovering over the white figure left on the ground.

Will was horrified. The dragon was about to destroy the Runemaster! The Gordin-dragon took a deep breath…

"Nooooo!" cried Will.

…and a ravening ball of fire consumed the figure and melted the stones on which it lay, leaving nothing but a pile of smoking ash and rubble.

Will leapt forward. His Quest had failed! The Runemaster was dead. Gordin had won! Nothing mattered now. The citizens of Dun Indewood – Lords, Counsellors, Knyghts, shopkeepers, servants and boys from the Knyght

School – peered from their hiding places in horrified fascination as the tiny figure swung his sword at the great beast, with no thought for his own safety.

Will slashed at the dragon's thigh. By sheer good fortune, the blade slid between the scales. Black dragon blood oozed, smoking, from the wound. The beast that had been Gordin gave a bellow of fury and swung its great head round to knock Will flying. His sword went spinning from his grasp.

Gyles, watching from an archway at the side of the square, snatched a round shield from the grasp of a petrified guard. "Here! Will!" With a flick of his wrist, he sent it spinning like a plate through the air. Will snatched and caught it. Even as he did so, he realised that it would be no protection from the heat of the dragon's fire. He heard the dragon draw breath again.

Instinctively, he rolled over and flung the shield at it.

The shield sliced through the air and wedged between the dragon's teeth as it lowered its head to belch fire. The flame blew back from the shield and flared round the dragon's head, turning it into a fireball. The crowd cheered.

Then the flame cleared. The dragon stood for a moment, half blinded, racked with pain and rooted in shock. Then it shook its injured head and gave a hiss of pure malice. It crunched the remains of the shield deliberately between its giant jaws. Its eyes narrowed. It was hurt, but not defeated. Will's last hope died.

He stood still, head bowed, waiting for the end. The

dragon reared above him and took a deep, triumphant breath.

At that moment, a great cry echoed across the piazza. "Greywing Draconis! I summon thee!"

On top of the wall on the other side of the square, stood a tall figure in grey robes.

It was the Runemaster. His hand was held aloft and in it blazed the Dragonsbane.

CHAPTER TWENTY-EIGHT

How, in the Heat of Battle, the High Lord Gordin fell from Grace.

With a thunder of wings, the Dragon of the Ragged Mountain appeared in answer to the Runemaster's call. Roaring defiance, Gordin the Man-Drake leapt up to meet it.

The cowering citizens of Dun Indewood watched in awe as the two dragons flew at each other. Each creature fired a jet of flame and each twisted out of the way. The adversaries climbed, banked, swooped and spun round each other in giddy spirals. Flashes of dragon-fire tore across the sky.

Will dragged his eyes from the conflict raging above him as Rose came running across the square towards him, followed by the Runemaster. He stared at the old man with wide-eyed amazement. "But you're dead... I saw..."

"It was a ruse, Will!" yelled Rose, straining to be heard above the roars of the furious dragons. "Humfrey and Luigi never had the Dragonsbane – I had it all the time! They put Gordin off the scent long enough for me to get to the Runemaster."

"But the body! I saw it! If it wasn't the Runemaster, who...?" They ducked as Greywing pulled out of a dive just above their heads and climbed back to the attack.

"Explanations later!" The Runemaster's voice was calm, but decisive. "I think we should get under cover, don't you?"

The battle continued to rage above them. Lord Gordin, the Man-Drake, was younger and faster than Greywing; but the Dragon of the Ragged Mountain had a lifetime of battle experience behind it. A cunning mid-air twist sent a jet of fire streaming across Gordin's flank. The younger dragon howled its fury and dived to the attack again.

Rose and Will crouched behind a stone buttress next to the Runemaster.

"Man-Drake!" the old man muttered. "It was staring me in the face all the time. How can I have been so blind?"

Will glanced at him. "What do you mean?"

"Drake is an old word for 'dragon'," said the Runemaster. "Now, I understand! Tarkwin was right. Gordin's family was indeed in thrall to dark forces. My master didn't steal the Dragonsbane – he took it from the City to stop it falling into the hands of that creature."

A near-miss above demolished part of a roof. Tiles clattered around them.

"So Humfrey was right," said Will slowly, "and so was the Harp. Gordin came to steal the Dragonsbane..."

"Yes, and when he found that he could not control it while my life force was inside, he was consumed with anger. The power of the Dragonsbane caused him to transform into the beast we see before us. I watched, trapped inside the stone, as the creature rampaged about my chamber; but before it thought to destroy me, the transformation ended."

The dragons spun in the sky above. Gordin was wounded, but Greywing was tiring. Dragon-fire began to find its target. Now there were screams of agony between the roars of anger. Gordin came up from beneath Greywing and scored a hit on the older dragon's belly. The Dragon of the Ragged Mountain howled and dived clear. Gordin shot in pursuit.

Will could do nothing. Greywing was losing. The Runemaster's words spun around in his head even as tears sprang to Will's eyes. The power of the Dragonsbane... Gordin consumed with anger... transformation into the dragon... but why had the transformation ended?

A sudden inspiration struck Will. He spun round to face the Runemaster. "Give me the Dragonsbane!"

The Runemaster hesitated, then he dropped the stone into Will's outstretched hand. Will gazed into the Dragonsbane, projecting his mind into the stone. *Greywing!* He put all his concentration into the thought. *Greywing!*

I hear thee! The dragon's answering thought was desperate. *I suffer.*

Don't fight! Will told it. *Break off. Climb! Make him chase you – go higher!*

Run? Never!

Do it! Will's thought was a command. *Trust me.*

I obey.

Will gasped as his mind left the stone and he staggered. Rose caught him, her face concerned. "Are you all right? You seemed to be in a trance. What have you done?"

Will recovered himself with an effort and pointed skywards. "Watch!"

Above them, the Dragon of the Ragged Mountain had turned tail on his pursuer. With a bellow of triumph, the Man-Drake turned to follow.

The true dragon climbed high into the air, with deliberate wingbeats, using all its vast experience to seek out columns of rising air. The man-dragon followed, threshing madly with its wings, bent only on coming to grips with its enemy. As the watchers on the ground stared, the younger dragon faltered. It was tiring quickly. Fear and doubt assailed it. Its fury was draining away...

The dragons must have been almost a thousand feet up when the transformation occurred. Without the power of its anger to sustain it, the Man-Drake reverted to human form. Gordin, High Lord of Dun Indewood, became a man again.

He was high above the City.

He no longer had the Dragonsbane.

With a scream of despair, the High Lord fell from the sky. Will and Rose turned away as Gordin's fall ended in the middle of the square.

The Harp whistled. "Now that's what I *call* a pizza." The Runemaster gave it a furious glare. "Yeah, you're right." The Harp's voice was unusually subdued. "Bad taste. Sorry."

The Runemaster walked slowly forward. He took off his cloak and draped it over what remained of the High Lord of Dun Indewood. He remained kneeling beside it, lost in thought.

Rose and Will crossed the square to join the Runemaster. Luigi and Humfrey followed. The Dragon of the Ragged Mountain glided down and landed on the portico of the Merchants' Hall, overlooking the square. Slowly, and with many cautious glances towards the dragon, the citizens of Dun Indewood came out of hiding and began to fill the piazza.

Will felt dazed. "I still don't understand this." He glanced at the Runemaster. "I saw the Dragon burn his body to ashes."

"No, Will." Rose made an effort to keep her voice light. "While you were fooling around with the dragon, Humfrey told me about the switch, so I said I'd take the Dragonsbane to the Runemaster while they created a diversion."

Will looked at her blankly. "Switch?"

"The Runemaster's body never left the castle."

Humfrey nodded. "Firsht rule of inqueshtigation. You

269

wanna hide shomething, hide it where nobody'sh gonna look for it."

Luigi nodded. "Tha's right. We took the statue of one of those ol' Kings, then we dusted the Runemaster with flour and put him in its place. Then we took the statue back to the restaurant and hid it in the flour bin."

A look of wonder dawned on Will's face. "So all the time Gordin's men were searching for the Runemaster's body, it was right there in the Great Hall looking down on the searchers."

Humfrey grinned. "Am I the besht in the biznish, or what?"

The Runemaster straightened up. "There are many stories to be told, no doubt," he said firmly, "and we will hear them all later. But now, we must make an ending here."

Will lifted the Dragonsbane. He gazed at it, then at his companions.

He spoke to the Runemaster. "You returned the stone to the City. Yet it left your hands. Rose and I recovered it and she returned it to you and brought you back to life."

The Runemaster gazed curiously at Will. He hesitated, then nodded.

Will turned to Rose. "Will you allow me to decide the stone's future?"

Rose's answer was immediate. "Yes, Will."

Will said simply, "Thank you." Then he raised his head, and called, "Greywing!"

There were screams. The citizens of Dun Indewood scattered once again as the great dragon leapt from its perch, circled the square once, and landed facing Will. It folded its wings and waited.

Will smiled. "You arrived very quickly when the Runemaster called."

"I thought upon thy words at our last parting." There was a glint of amusement in the dragon's great, golden eye. *"Thou spakest true – if that creature had gained power over the stone, there would have been no refuge anywhere. I waited in the Forest nearby – until thou hadst need of me."*

"Gordin wanted the Dragonsbane so that he could force all the dragons to bring him their hoards. He wanted their gold."

The dragon lowered its head. *"His greed destroyed him."*

Will held out the Dragonsbane. "You told me that you had never been a man," he said clearly, "and were no longer a dragon. You told me that trust was a sacred thing. Will *you* take the stone?"

There were gasps and mutters from the crowd. The Runemaster started forward, opened his mouth to speak – and closed it again.

"I ask you to take the Dragonsbane," Will went on, "because you would not use it to turn men against dragons, or dragons against men. I charge you to keep it in your hoard and guard it, so that no less worthy a creature may use it for evil."

"I shall." The dragon said nothing more, but stretched out its long neck. Will reached up with the chain from which the Dragonsbane hung and fastened it around the narrowest part.

The dragon raised its head and then lowered it again in a slow, respectful bow, as to an equal. Then it opened its mighty wings and leapt skyward. Within a few wingbeats it had dwindled to a speck in the distance; then it was gone.

The Runemaster stepped forward and took Will by the shoulder. Wondering, Will followed the old man across the square. People flowed back behind them. The Runemaster led Will up the stone steps of the Merchants' Hall and turned to face the crowd.

The old man held up his arms. His voice rang across the square. "People of Dun Indewood. Your High Lord is dead! The City must elect a new ruler." The Runemaster indicated Will, who was staring back at him with a mixture of disbelief and horror. "He stands before you. Will has suffered from Gordin's tyranny. He has been wrongfully accused and proved his innocence. He has saved my life. In deciding the fate of the Dragonsbane, he has shown the wisdom of his judgement.

"His origins may be humble. He may be only a swineherd, but he has shown a nobility to put those of gentler birth to shame. He braved the dangers of the Forest to complete his Quest and saved the City."

The Runemaster spread his arms wide. "Ask yourselves!" he thundered. "Who would you have to lead you? Another greedy, forsworn and disgraced Lord like Gordin, or a man of honour? A dragonfriend? A hero? A Good Knyght? Citizens of Dun Indewood, what say you?"

CHAPTER TWENTY-NINE

How a Good Knyght said Goodbye, and
how this Book Ended, and the Others
Began...

"Great going, Runey," sneered the Harp. "It takes a special kind of loser to snatch defeat from the jaws of victory!"

The Runemaster shook his head sadly. "I could have sworn I had them all in the palm of my hand."

Will, Rose, Luigi, Humfrey and the Runemaster were sitting, rather crestfallen, in Rose's cottage.

Rose stood up and clapped her hands. "I know," she said with a ghastly attempt at brightness, "who'd like some nice moss broth?" There was a complete lack of eager agreement. "Please yourselves," Rose muttered and sat down again.

Luigi snapped his fingers. "'Ow about pizza?"

Four pairs of eyes glared at him.

"Jus' a thought," said Luigi hastily. "Jus' a thought."

The citizens of Dun Indewood had cheered the Runemaster's speech, given Will a unanimous and heartfelt vote of thanks for rescuing them from the tyranny of Gordin, and then unanimously elected Lord Robat fitzBadley as the new High Lord.

"Why did they choose that old bumbler?" pondered Humfrey. "Humansh – shtrange creaturesh."

"Not really," said Rose despondently. "People want comfort and an easy life. They'll get that with Robat all right. He doesn't know what day of the week it is half the time." She sighed. "People don't want heroes. They're *different*. Heroes rock the boat. They do exciting things, they visit dangerous places, and that's the problem. Heroes make most people think their own lives are pretty boring and meaningless."

"But heroes is like sauce on a dish a' pasta. You gotta have some, otherwise i's all dry and tasteless," argued Luigi.

"What is this?" cried the Harp. "A cookery course? Listen up; it's all very simple: they wanted Robat, they didn't want the pig-fancier. End of menu! Agh! Now you've got me doing it!"

"Ah, well," said Rose. "At least they didn't choose Symon."

"Perhaps Symon is to be pitied," said the Runemaster. "He may be a worthless wretch, but he did not know what his father truly was. Now he is fatherless – and Cityless, exiled forever from Dun Indewood."

The Harp raised its voice in sarcastic song:

> *"Daddy's a dragon, my life's turned around*
> *Since Daddy came down and went splat on the ground.*
> *Hush, hush! Nobody cares*
> *Symon is going to get eaten by bears…*

…or maybe foxes – or maybe snakes. Maybe squirrels even. Let's look on the bright side."

"Exactly," said Will with forced cheerfulness. "Look on the bright side. Being High Lord wouldn't have suited me at all. Just think of all those things I'd have had to do, like having to go to dozens of feasts and banquets…" (He looked ruefully at the green slop bubbling away in the pot over the fire.) "Live in a castle… Have people running after me, obeying my every word… Doing whatever I wanted to do, whenever I wanted to do it…" He sighed. "It would have been awful."

"Yeah, absolutely terrible," the Harp retorted. "Keep on saying it and one day you'll believe it."

"So what happens next?" asked Will.

"Well, I gotta restaurant to run," replied Luigi. "I gotta idea for a new dish: Pasta alla Fuoco. I's green pasta in the shape of a dragon, topped with a chilli an' pepper sauce that'll burn your tongue off."

"It'sh not my tongue I'd be worried about," Humfrey muttered darkly. He turned to the Runemaster. "What about you, Popsh? What'sh your next move?"

The Runemaster sighed mournfully. "I am at a loss to

know. I have cast the runes, but all they show is mystery. I do not understand it."

"Myshtery, hey?" drawled Humfrey. "Maybe I can anshwer that one."

The Runemaster gave him a puzzled stare.

"Now Gordin'sh gone and boggartsh, elvesh, dwarvesh, etshetera, etshetera are being allowed back into Dun Indewood, I can go legitimate as a Private Inqueshtigator. I'm gonna shet up an office, get a shecretary and make a killing... In the money shenshe," Humfrey added quickly.

"And what does this venture have to do with me?" asked the Runemaster.

"I'll need help. Those runesh of yoursh could be great for biznish. I can shee it now...

Boggart and Rune
Pryvate Inqueshtigatorsh
Crimesh sholved before they happen.

It'll have the puntersh pouring in," grinned Humfrey. He held out his hand. "How about it? Partnersh?"

The Runemaster thought for a moment. He looked at the others. Rose, Will and Luigi were grinning. Will nodded encouragingly. The Runemaster shrugged and took Humfrey's outstretched hand. "Partners."

Humfrey slapped his new partner on the back. "Runey, I think thish ish the beginning of a beautiful friendship."

Symon struggled through the undergrowth of the Forest, sniffling and muttering to himself.

It had been a bad twenty-four hours. He'd found out his dad was a dragon, he'd become an orphan (which hadn't really bothered him as he'd never liked his dad much), he'd been expelled from the Knyght School, and (this REALLY annoyed him) he'd been stripped of his titles and banished from Dun Indewood.

Symon's mind was a whirl of hatred and self-pity. Spite welled up inside him like a living force. Let them banish him! They'd be sorry. He would survive. No, he would do more than survive! He would build himself a shelter (he was sure he'd read a book on this once... or at least looked at the pictures... or at least meant to). Then he would hunt down some prey (something that couldn't run fast and didn't bite or scratch too much). He would become strong and plot his revenge.

How dare the scum of Dun Indewood strip him of his titles! Revenge! He would bring together the creatures of the Dark Forest. He would teach them how to stand up for his rights! He would turn them into an invincible army. Revenge! He would be their great general. He would lead them to Dun Indewood, tear down the walls, take over the City and claim back his rightful position. Revenge! And as for Willum the pig boy and his degenerate, treacherous friends – well, they'd be very sorry they ever messed with Symon Mandrake. Revenge, revenge, REVENGE!

Symon's smile was nuttier than a squirrel's breakfast as he thought of the incredibly nasty things he would do to get his own back. His revenge would be sweeter than a bee's banquet, sharper than a weasel's teeth, more terrible than... more terrible... more...

His thoughts were interrupted by a strange odour that drifted through the Forest air.

Symon sniffed and frowned. There was a very strong doggy smell.

There was a sound of panting right in his ear. Small drops of saliva splattered on to his arm. Symon trembled. He felt hot breath on the back of his neck.

"Well, helloooo..."

Will and Rose escorted their friends back to Dun Indewood before the City gates closed for the night. Luigi, Humfrey and the Runemaster said their goodbyes. Rolph, the guard, watched them go in and turned to Will.

"Evenin', Will, coming in tonight?"

Will looked up at the City walls. He looked back at the Forest. Slowly, he shook his head.

"Righto, mind how you go." Rolph patted Will on the shoulder and stepped back through the gate. It closed behind him.

Rose gave Will a searching look. "Aren't you going back to the Knyght School?"

Will shook his head. "There's more to being a Good Knyght than going to the right school. A Good Knyght isn't just something you call yourself, it's something you *are* – or try to be."

As he and Rose walked back towards the Forest, Will gave a deep sigh. "So, what was it all about?"

Rose gave him an odd look. "I think it was about you becoming a Good Knyght."

"You think so?" Will shook his head. "All I seemed to do was end up being on the menu of every creature we ever met. You were the one who got me out of all those scrapes."

Rose suddenly seemed to find her feet very interesting. "It was teamwork," she said. "We all defeated Gordin. And you fulfilled your destiny. I suppose," she added uncertainly.

Will gazed back at the City. "Did I? Oh, good." He turned to Rose. "But what happens now? What happens when you've done what you were supposed to have done? What happens with the rest of my life?"

The Harp chirped up. "Like it says in the books, we all live happily ever after."

"What does that mean? I just fade away and do nothing?"

"Maybe your destiny is feeding pigs," suggested the Harp.

Will ignored the instrument's jibe. He remembered the

dragon-flight with Greywing. He could recall the vast expanse of the Dark Forest and the glimpses of other cities. If there really was no end to the Dark Forest, there could be anything out there. Anything.

Will turned and faced the Forest. "Maybe my destiny is to keep searching for my destiny."

The Harp gave a puzzled twang. "I was with you right up to 'maybe'."

"What I'm saying is... I think I'll leave Dun Indewood and go exploring. How about it, Harp?"

The Harp's strings hummed with horror. "Are you crazy? You expect me to go back into that jungle? Has the fight with the big reptile turned you completely ga ga?"

"Too bad you feel that way," mused Will. "I'll just have to leave you here with Rose."

"Her!" shrieked the Harp. "Of course I'm coming into the Forest with you. It'll be an honour! A privilege, even!"

"That's settled then."

Rose smiled. "That'll be lovely. A nice trip in the Forest, just the three of us..."

"Three?" The Harp quivered with worry. "I think you've got your sums wrong here, lady. Me and him makes two."

Rose raised an eyebrow at Will. "You don't think I'm going to let you go off wandering into the Forest on your own?"

Will smiled. "Are you sure?"

Rose nodded. "Certain."

"Not the girl," wailed the Harp. "How am I supposed to live happily ever after if she..." The Harp's moans were cut off as Rose unceremoniously dumped the instrument into its bag – face first.

Will grinned. "OK." He started walking towards the Forest. "Let's go and see what else is out there."

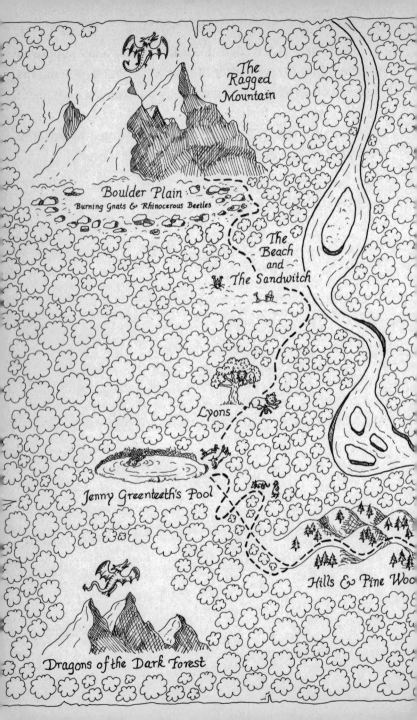

The Ragged Mountain

Boulder Plain
Burning Gnats & Rhinocerous Beetles

The Beach and The Sandwitch

Lyons

Jenny Greenteeth's Pool

Hills & Pine Woo

Dragons of the Dark Forest

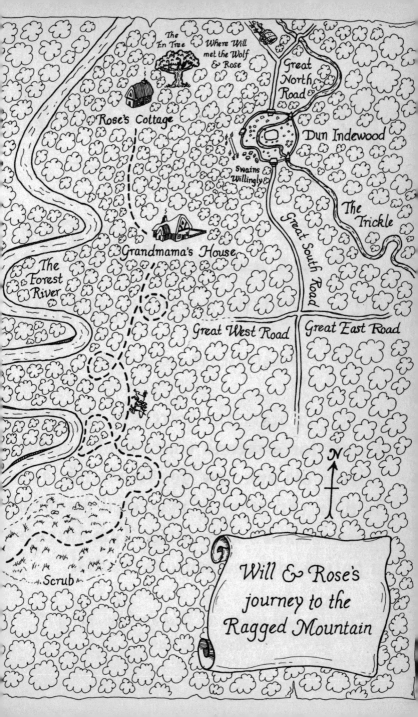

Sproutyng soone

TALES OF THE DARK FOREST

WHIZZARD!

STEVE BARLOW & STEVE SKIDMORE

ILLUSTRATED BY FIONA LAND

Dare you brave the secrets of the Dark Forest for a second time? Look out for friends old and new, for fiends fair and foul, in this story of magyckal mayhem when wizard's apprentice Tym invents a potion with momentous results!

"Fashten your sheatbelts - thish one'sh a shcorcher!"
Boggart Tribune